To Kaitlyn

THEIRS TO LOVE

DOMS OF CRAVE COUNTY: BOOK ONE

ABIGAIL LEE JUSTICE

Keep it Kinky
Abigail Lee
Justice
xoxo

THEIRS TO LOVE © October2015 by Abigail Lee Justice

All rights reserved. No part of this book may be reproduced, scanned, or distributed in any printed or electronic form without permission. Please do not participate in or encourage piracy of copyrighted materials in violation of the author's rights.

This is a work of fiction. Names, places, characters, and incidents are the product of the author's imagination and are fictitious. Any resemblance to actual persons, living or dead, events, or establishments is solely coincidental. All sexually active characters in this work are 18 years of age or older.

This book is for sale to ADULT AUDIENCES ONLY. It contains substantial sexually explicit scenes and graphic language which may be considered offensive by some readers. Please store your files where they cannot be access by minors.

Cover design by: Bethany Cagle

Images used under appropriate license from 123rf.com.

Warning the unauthorized reproduction or distributions of this copyright work is illegal. Criminal copyright infringements, including infringement without monetary gain, is investigated by the FBI and is punishable by up 5 years in prison and a fine of $250,000.

ACKNOWLEDGEMENTS

To the very creative and talented wordsmith, Brynna Curry, your calming words during our many phone conversations put my mind at ease night after night after I hung up with you. Without your kind words of encouragements, fine tweaking, and most of all your knowledge of writing and editing, I'm most sure this book would have stayed on my iPad forever without being published. Thank you from the bottom of my heart.

Special thanks goes out to my beta readers, Lisa, Jenn, and slave Tara, without the bantering back and forth, this book would still be locked away in my mind.

To my loving parents, my sons, in-laws, family, friends and especially readers, you all are very near and dear to me. Without all of your guidance and support, I wouldn't have become the person I am today. Thank you.

To Orja, when I first read your poem a few years ago, I never dreamed that it would be the final puzzle for reshaping my life. Your words strengthened me. Each day is a new chapter in my amazing journey. Thank you for allowing me to publish "Surrender" in my books.

To my loving husband, this book is dedicated to you. Your support these past 30 years together has had its ups and downs, you've always supported me in everything I've ever done and this book was no exception. For sleepless nights, cursing and swearing, crazy computer issues, weekends away from home attending cons and book signings, thank you from the bottom of my slave's heart. SRD: I love you :) PG..

CHAPTER 1

Christ, it is hotter than the fucking Sahara Desert in this blasted restaurant. Sitting at the long tile countertop, Charlotte Maxwell wondered what the hell she was doing in Crave County after all these years instead of her swanky New York apartment. She tapped her finger to the sound of the jukebox she'd turned on for company in the empty room.

Charlotte stared at her coffee mug, which read, "A good diner has open doors, opened arms, and open hearts." *Why did you need to have all these sappy sayings everywhere, Mom?*

Sweat trickled down her forehead, under her hairline, down her back, soaking her bra and panties. Sighing she looked around the old run-down diner and considered what her next move would be. *Broken air conditioner. Great. Shit, I truly can't take another problem.* So many problems lumped on top of thousands she had inherited from her parents.

Feeling slightly more pissed then she had yesterday after having the grill fixed, she faced yet another hurdle. Looking up to the heavens, Charlie closed her eyes. *Mom, I really need you now. Send me some kind of sign. Help me fix the shit that keeps on piling up. I so need your help.*

It had already been a long morning, she needed more caffeine to survive, but it was just too hot for coffee, so instead she settled for iced tea. Hopefully, it would give her the jolt she needed to get her ass in gear. She'd skipped breakfast again this morning. It had become her usual habit. Hell, skipping most meals was the norm for Charlotte.

Without really thinking, she picked up her mother's handy dandy address book listing all of the companies her mother had used in the past to maintain the business. Smack dab in the middle of the page under HVAC was the name and number for Ryder Repairs. Without overthinking her options, Charlie dialed the number, prepared to leave a message.

After the second ring, a deep baritone voice answered,

"Hello, Ryder Repair, Mac here. How may I help you?"

Startled that someone actually answered the phone; her mousy voice surprised her as if she had just heard a ghost.

"Hi, this is Charlotte Maxwell over at Maxwell's Diner. I was wondering if...well." Taken by surprise, Charlotte couldn't get her voice to work.

"Charlie? You still there?"

Feeling like such a fool, she blurted out, "I am checking to see if you have any last minute cancellations today. I think something is wrong with our air-conditioning unit."

"Tell me what the unit is doing exactly."

"Well, for starters, when I opened up the restaurant this morning, it felt as if the temperature were a hundred degrees already. That's without turning any of the appliances on."

"Ok, tell me more. Is it hissing or leaking anything from the compressor?"

"Let me check." Charlotte walked outside where the compressor unit sat on a concrete slab; nothing seemed to be leaking from the vents. The fan blades were rotating round and round. No abnormal hissing noises were coming from the unit. She relayed the same to Ryder.

"No, not as far as I can tell. I checked the thermostat again before deciding to call in the cavalry. It registered eighty-five. I turned it down to seventy and now it's reading ninety."

Mackenzie Ryder had been the football star in high school. He was every girls wet dream back in those days, tall, dark black hair, blue eyes, fit and trim body, the kind you could bounce a quarter off of his stomach muscles. She was as flustered now as she had been back then.

Fuck, it has been forever since I thought about Mr. Sex Walking.

It was common knowledge if you went out on a date with Mackenzie; you got a two for one deal. Double your pleasure, double the fun. Dillon, Mackenzie's twin brother, was the other half of the package deal. She couldn't remember a time when they dated separately. They always dated the same girl at the same time. Hence, double the fun. Most of her friends came from a polygamous upbringing. It was nothing new to the people who lived in Crave County.

I wonder if they are settled down now. Hell, what could be so special about those two big, dominant, possessive, hunks that they wouldn't be settled down now.

Every one of her other friends were in committed relationships, why would these two be any different? Just hearing his voice made her go all gooey inside and put her in a daze. She felt her panties dampen. Taking another drink to quench her thirst, she slowly pressed the glass to her lips hoping Mac couldn't hear her wetting her whistle.

Secretly she'd had a crush on both Mac and Dillon back in high school, but she always stayed as far off their radar as possible. Knowing that she was way out of their league, Charlotte tried to keep her fantasies locked away. Would she still be out of her league?

"Give me just a minute; let me take a look at the schedule."

She began tapping her fingernails nervously on the counter, trying not to get too excited about Mac answering the call to come out and save the day. Wonderful, he would be her cavalry, her white knight in shining armor.

After only a few seconds, she heard Mac say, "Let's see now. Yep. I have a house call at the O'Malley place at nine to replace her thermostat, which should take me about ten minutes to install. Knowing old lady O'Malley, she'll want to feed me some of her famous lemon poppy seed cake. Which is mouthwatering by the way, but not as good as your mom's was."

"Yeah she did make the best desserts in town." Feeling tears well up, she realized she hadn't let her emotions flow since her parents' passing. "I am grateful she was able to publish her cookbook before she died; now everyone can still have a piece of mom's yummy goodies. Sorry for being such a buzz kill. It's just hard to think about how my mom won't be baking anymore."

"No, Charlie, it's good to talk about your parents. You're still grieving. I'm not sure how I would handle losing my parents all of sudden. Shit, just being dumped on as you've been would make me go crazy. At least I have Dillon to lean on. You only have your Aunt Trudy."

"Yeah this really sucks big time. I never envisioned myself back in Crave after all these years. Hopefully it won't be long before I can head back to New York." Charlie let out a huge sigh as she let the words roll off her tongue. She really wasn't sure if she missed New York or if she just needed the comfort of not being in Crave.

"Dillon took the day off to go fishing, which leaves me all by my lonesome. Normally, you'd get a twofer but today I'm going solo."

Wow, just hearing she was missing a twofer made her lose sight of the conversation with the rock solid hunk on the other end of the line.

"How does ten o'clock sound for you?"

"Perfect. I hope that you can get some air circulating before the lunch crowd comes billowing in. I'd hate to have everyone eat their lunch being all hot and sticky."

"We can't have that. Now can we?"

"No. At the rate I'm going, by the time you get here you just might find me in a puddle of water melted away like the wicked witch of west from the Wizard of Oz." She giggled. It had been a long time since she laughed aloud. She couldn't even remember the last time she let a joke slip.

"Now, now, sweetheart. I can't have you melting. The last time that I saw you, if I'm not mistaken, your face was the perfect color of a cream puff, and not that old wrinkled, wart infested green color."

"Mac, you're so funny." For the first time in a long time, she felt herself let go. She even felt a little tingly inside. Another thing she remembered about the Ryder twins, they were funny as hell. They loved to play practical jokes on just about everyone.

She remembered going to the local swimming hole for an afternoon or evening dip with the rest of their friends wasn't out of the norm on a hot summer's day.

Jackson Hole was the hot spot to go skinny-dipping; all the locals did including Charlie. Having the Ryder twins steal everyone clothes was another story in itself. They liked the look of sheer and utter shock on the girls' faces when they got out of the water and had nothing to wear. Real perverts the two of them.

One summer evening Charlie arrived late for a quick dip with the rest of her friends. She saw Mac taking everyone's clothes and hiding them in a tree. Brushing her hand over her mouth in utter shock, Charlie realized she had a secret, something she could hold over Mac and she did. Keeping it quiet for all these years.

Instead, whenever the subject of the missing clothes came up, the Ryder brothers made up some crazy ass story about how big foot must have stolen them. Having secretly liked both of the Ryder brothers, Charlie never said a thing. When she was face to face with them, she felt a little ache straight down to her pussy.

That's exactly how she felt now, just talking to this gorgeous guy. That little twitch began between her legs.

Not all of her memories of growing up were bad; it was only one memory that had left her heart scarred for life.

"Charlie, you still there?"

Silence had filled the air last few seconds. "Oh sorry, I was just remembering how we all used to go to Jackson Hole on a hot summer afternoon."

"Those were the days, weren't they? God, such great memories. If only we could go back in time."

Her heart began to race at the thought. She needed to end this call before she started to drool over the phone, or she said something that just might get her libido hyped up.

"Ok, I guess I'll see you at ten."

"Don't worry. I'll have you cooled down in no time." *I'd rather you heat me up.* She had a few dirty thoughts running through her brain.

"Are you sure about that?"

"Oh I think so. Later, sweetheart."

As she hung up the phone, she heard some of the kitchen staff milling around. Maybe her day wasn't going to turn out so bad after all.

Damn, she'd been used to having some bad days and nights over the past few years. She needed a little sparkle of hope every now and then. *Maybe today is the day!*

She couldn't concentrate on anything, except for the memory of Mackenzie Ryder's sexy ass voice. Now she was more hot and bothered than she had been few minutes ago. Her body was a burning little furnace of unexpected desire and she still had to start the morning cleaning process.

For it only being the beginning of July, damn I'm hot. Or am I hot and bothered by the recent phone call with Mac Ryder?

She ran her hands up and down her sides, trying to get some of the moisture off her sweating fingers. Charlotte knew that keeping the diner opened would cause not only a financial burden to her, but it would also require her to make a drastic change in living arrangements.

Am I ready to make that decision today? Fuck, did I just have that thought?

What would her next move be?

It had been nearly three months since her parents died in a horrible car accident. How much longer would she actually keep up pretending that everything was okay in her life? With the bills pilling up from her parents' estate, Charlie was sure looking at hard times.

Her parents had a small amount of money put aside, but nothing that would sustain running a diner.

Leaving everything in their will to Charlotte had been a huge surprise to her, since she'd helped her parents write up their will only a few years back, naming her Aunt Trudy as the beneficiary.

She should have been out of the picture completely, but something must have changed Charlie's parents mind forcing them to change Aunt Trudy's name to hers without even telling her. They must have had a plan for her.

Maxwell's Diner was the biggest money pit in the world. Now it was all hers. Remembering the advice her father gave her many, many years ago, she said aloud, "with a lot of hard work you can make anything work." That's exactly what her parents did. They'd turned the restaurant into a well-liked establishment that everyone who lived in Crave County loved.

It took the Maxwells five years to make magic happen. Devotion to their patrons was one thing that made the restaurant successful but it was also the hot spot for the townspeople to learn gossip about everything going on in Crave.

More or less, the long days and nights made Maxwell's Diner what it was today.

The sooner I sell the diner, the sooner I can high tail it back to my life in New York. If I stay, could I find happiness?

Every night for the past three months, she had dreamt of nothing else. How could she sell the diner that brought her family so much joy for the past twenty years? Even though it had never been Charlie's desire to run the diner, she did enjoy working at the diner as a teenager during her summer break. It held special memories of her past that weren't so bad at all.

Being totally a daddy's girl, she loved the extra time she spent with her father. It nearly broke her heart when she made the decision to go away for college, but she knew it was the only way she was going to escape her past, even if it meant breaking her father's heart. If it hadn't been for the weekly calls to her parents, Charlie would have been deeply depressed. The small talk kept her from tipping over the edge.

Charlotte was no longer that skinny, red-haired, freckled faced girl, now she was a woman who was totally lost. She was no longer the fiery, loud mouth, whirlwind girl of Crave County. She had never seen herself as sexy or even attractive. She was damaged goods. Not good for any man.

When she looked in the mirror, she saw a single, withdrawn, pale, curvy woman who hadn't had a steady boyfriend since high school. Most of her friends from Crave either were in a serious relationship or settled down with their childhood sweethearts.

Not Charlotte, she was still single at the age of twenty-six with no hope of settling down in the near future. She often dreamed of the white picket fence, two kids, two cars in the garage deal, but what man or men would ever take on a used woman?

None she had ever met.

Even her best friend Justine had tied the knot almost a year ago to the Murray brothers. She had landed herself three of the nicest guys in the entire town, well except for the Ryder twins.

Why did her mind keep remembering the guys that turned her on? They wouldn't want a damaged girl. She would still be a virgin if it not for that ill-fated night. That is what coursed through her every waking moment since returning to Crave. She hated that she couldn't just turn her brain off and forget about Carl Hugh.

She shuttered every time she silently said his name. *Now's not the time to be thinking about that slime ball.* Not even Justine knew about douche bag Carl.

Trying to pull herself out of that horror picture, Charlotte refocused her thoughts about her future. Could she plot her big exit plan without stirring up emotions from the townspeople of Crave? Everyone had been super supportive during her time of grief. She hated disappointing them now, especially Justine, who was seven months pregnant with triplets and had asked Charlie to be the triplet's godmother. Reluctantly, she hadn't given Justine an answer yet. Getting attached was not in the picture for her.

Forever.

Growing up in a small rural Pennsylvania town, where everybody knew everything about everyone had been rewarding up until that fated day in November eight years ago.

Charlotte couldn't get that picture out of her mind. Unfortunately for her it had been etched in her brain forever. It haunted her every single day. Even though only her Aunt Trudy and her therapist new her secret, she always feared that somehow, someone would find out.

She could picture the billboard sign welcoming new comers to the town.

Welcome to Crave County, where all walks of life are welcome, except for Charlie Maxwell who was DAMAGED GOODS!

That wasn't the kind of sign visitors wanted to read. No matter how much booze she ingested, money she spent on counseling, Charlotte would always feel like a piece of her was missing, taken forcibly from her.

Watching everyone's life around her move on, day-by-day, she felt stuck in sort of a vortex that just kept spinning out of control. It was easier to hide in New York because no one knew her horrible secret. Not even her closest friend in New York, Milly Stafford, knew. Her friends were business partners that got together after a long day at the firm for a drink. Most of the time they continued discussing their caseloads or important case related information. None were true girlfriend material. Just business associates.

Being a junior lawyer in one of New York's finest law firms had always been Charlotte's dream. When that dream final came true, she thought she was actually free and clear of her past.

CHAPTER 2

She realized she had been sadly mistaken when she thought escape was the answer but her worries followed her to New York. Countless sessions with her psychologist had broken down part of the emotional wall she had built. She still hadn't released her mind to love again. She needed to be free of her past. Could she just let it go?

Charlotte knew that eventually she would have to face her fears. She never thought that day would come when she was called back to Crave to deal with the loss of her parents. Facing her fears was becoming more and more impossible.

After receiving the call from the Arizona State Highway patrol telling her about the accident, she had done everything possible not to come back to Crave, even going as far as trying to have her parents buried back in New York, but her mother's sister, Trudy St. Clair, immediately stopped that.

Not even Charlotte's knowledge of the laws about wills could stop Aunt Trudy from convincing Charlotte to return to Crave County.

Aunt Trudy was more than just Charlotte's loving aunt; she was in every sense of the word a second mother. Whenever Charlotte had issues that couldn't be shared with her mother, she found herself confiding in Aunt Trudy, even down to the secret she'd locked away. Not even Charlotte's parents knew.

Trudy was everyone's aunt in Crave County. She was bold, crass, and fearsome. Even as a small child Charlotte remembered hearing her parents talk to Aunt Trudy telling her if anything ever happened to them their wishes were to be buried together all three of them on top of Crave Mountain, overlooking everyone in Crave County. They also placed Aunt Trudy as her guardian until she reached eighteen.

Charlotte never saw herself ever settling down as her parents had. Living the dream through her parent's eyes would be the best Charlie could do. Her parents shared something that most families in Crave shared, having multiple spouses.

Her mother told her it was the norm in Crave County to have multiple spouses. She could still hear her mother's voice telling her, 'Someday, Charlotte, you may find yourself sandwiched between two, three, or even four men and loving it."

Charlotte just shook her head as she let those words ring into her ears. *Not if she could help it.*

Growing up in Crave the norm was to have either multiple fathers, or multiple mothers. In Charlotte's case, she'd been blessed with two loving, kind and caring dads, who happened to be brothers. The Maxwell household was just like any other modern day household except two men loved her mother. Charlotte had been brought up in a polyamory society. Most of the families were made up of two, three, four, or five partners.

She was fortunate that both of her fathers worked for the local law enforcement, allowing her mother to be a stay at home mom. When Charlotte was ten years old, Daddy Samuel was shot while chasing down a bank robber.

Apprehending criminals after Daddy Samuel was shot had been the sole job of Charlotte's other father, Daddy Paul. Samuel had been forced to leave the police department after losing the ability to hold a gun, let alone shoot under duress.

What it had done for the Maxwell family though was give her family the time to open up Maxwell's Diner.

At first, when the diner first opened, Charlotte's mom, Norma, baked pies from their home, while Daddy Samuel built the restaurant brick by brick, making it the only diner in Crave County.

After several years of sweat, tears, and hard work, Norma joined her husband three days a week and cooked fantastic dishes for many of the townspeople.

Once Charlotte left Crave County, her mom would Skype with her weekly, filling her in on what had happened during the week at the diner and the other local gossip. The kind of stuff that Charlie didn't want to be reminded about. She loved speaking with her mother but it also brought sadness.

Seeing the excitement all over her mom's face said life in Crave for them was happy and fulfilling. She knew her parents had been truly happy with how they raised her. It didn't matter if she had one father or ten Charlotte loved her parents.

Now standing in the very spot that her mother once stood sent chills up and down Charlotte's neck. Looking around the diner, she had to face reality. Before her mind swirled deeper into thought, she had to pull herself together and act like an adult. Trying not to act like anything was wrong, Charlotte went about calculating last night's dinner tickets.

Her mother had a ledger for everything, she wasn't sure how they had survived without a bookkeeping system on a computer, but it had worked for many years for them.

This will surely not work for me. I need to have the records on a fucking computer not a book that could get lost. Another project that needs to be done. Fuck, did I just think that? I was going to make changes to keep this place. I must be delusional or having heat stroke because of the increasing temperature. Fear spiked through her veins.

Fuck, fuck a duck. I must be crazy just thinking the unthinkable. Keeping the diner was a huge step. Was she ready to let her trepidations take over her again?

Dark, ugly panic twisted and turned making her pulse race. *I'm a fucking lawyer for god's sake not a restaurant owner.* She felt her pulse really start to speed up when all she kept thinking about was how she could survive this terrible dilemma. The thought of leaving Crave again fucking made her heart hurt. She'd leave behind her Aunt Trudy this time and the memories of her parents. She'd had the same feeling, the night before she left for law school.

The thought crept back to light again about never settling down, never having a family, never having someone that loved her for who she was made her heart clinch. She'd feel better once she was settled back in her apartment. Why did life have to be so fucking confusing?

"Earth to Charlie. Come in Charlie! Hey are you all right, Charlie?" Looking a little puzzled, Charlie turned her head and saw Gloria, one of the waitresses, staring at her.

Having everyone stay on had been a godsend. Since she knew very little about running the diner, she had to rely on the staff and her Aunt Trudy.

"Oh God, how long have you been standing in front of me waiting for a response?"

"Only a few seconds. Are you okay, Hun? Your face is all flustered, your shirt is soaked, and you look like you're ready to have a stroke."

Just as Gloria got her last words out of her mouth, Charlie felt the room spinning, her stomach did a twist, and her body was on fire. She closed her eyes, fought the darkness and that's all she wrote.

"Charlie. Charlie! Wake up, Hun." Gloria shouted out to one of the kitchen cooks. "Go get Doc Owens. Charlie passed out. Greg, call Aunt Trudy, tell her to get her ass over here now."

Running as fast as she could, Gloria got a cool towel and placed it under Charlotte's neck until help arrived.

CHAPTER 3

Puttering around in the small workshop, Mackenzie Ryder had little to no spare time before his first service call of the day. He loved walking around, knowing that everything under the roof of small shop had been all from the hard work his fathers had endure the first few years in Crave County.

Knowing that he was all alone in the warehouse, Mac meandered around every morning just like today, until the rest of his employees showed up for work.

Tinkering about from aisle to aisle gave him some extra time to himself, that's why he didn't mind opening up at six a.m. Mac loved seeing all the signs his fathers had handmade when they first started the business nearly forty years ago. Everything that Ryder Repair stood for back in the day, both Mac and Dillon tried to preserve even as far as keeping traditions alive in the family business.

Every customer was treated with kid gloves. He needed to please the customers as much as possible. It echoed throughout the warehouse walls.

Once both Mac and Dillon returned from college, the business was handed over to them. They shared equal ownership rights to Ryder Repairs because being twins they often shared just about everything. And when they said everything, they meant everything, including their woman.

It had been Mac's dads Colton and Dustin Ryder's dream to open up the first and only air conditioning repair shop in Crave County all those years ago.

His dads were one of the founding members of Crave County, along with the Maxwell, Zellar, Murray and Schmidt families many years back.

Being amongst a diverse group of people, Colton and Dustin Ryder sought out a parasol of land large enough that several other families could purchase and set up a town completely run by the townspeople.

Forty years ago, land wasn't hard to come by; all you needed was a little money, knowledge, and the skills to create a working township. Thankfully, Mac's grandparents came from an aristocratic upbringing, leaving them with enough money to buy up several towns.

They used some of their inheritance to buy the land known as Crave County. Separating the land into sizable plots was left up to the Zellar family. With the land divided up, Crave County was born.

Horace Zellar's love and passion for finding agriculture rich in minerals made Crave County a wonderful place to farm crops, raise animals and it provided natural source of pure water. Everything a family would need.

At first, many obstacles had to be overcome, but as time went by, the town was completely run by a board of directors. If a potential new family wanted to come and live in Crave, they had to show just cause, or how they could help the town of Crave grow. Several areas had been set aside for newcomers to Crave.

Basically, Crave was a small rural town full of kinky people. Most of them weren't accepted by society because of their sexual proclivities. It was something everyone from Crave had been affected by one way or another.

No one living in Crave was considered an outcast or perverts because of their sexual taste. Everyone was free to be who they were. All lifestyles were accepted in Crave County.

Love was all that mattered in Crave and there was plenty of that going on. Most members socialized at Maxwell's or the local BDSM club called The FARM, owned and operated by Kyle Zeller who took over ownership from his grandfather Horace Zeller. Even though he didn't live in Crave County, he and his family being one of the founding families frequently visited the club monthly.

Mac loved being able to express his dominance. He had learned from the very best when doing his training several years back at The Farm.

Many of the submissives coming to The Farm loved being able to scene with the Ryder twins. Giving a submissive what she needed was all Mac and Dillon wanted and in return, they required their woman's full submission. D/s lifestyle was a give and take between all parties.

Recently, they had felt something was missing from their life. Settling down was the big elephant in the room for the two of them. Why had they not found their perfect little submissive yet? This had been the hot topic between the two of them for the past six months. Both had crushes on women from their high school days but none of them held a candle to one special woman, Charlie Maxwell.

They knew that one day she would return to their hometown. Neither brother thought it would be on such a sad note of losing her parents. They would need to pull out all their charms to win their girl.

He and Dillon had only a few serious relationships during the past couple years, but none had worked out. Secretly they'd had a crush on Charlie during high school but hadn't pursued their desires. Her name was always on the tip of their tongues but neither of the two ever brought the subject up. Every-time they saw Charlie Maxwell she was never alone, she always had a gaggle of Chatty Cathy girls at her side, which left them out in the cold. Even being two years older than she was, they all seemed to hang in the same circle of friends.

Getting a phone call from her this morning was like receiving a message from above. Could this be the sign that both of them had been waiting for? Shaking his head from side to side, it gave Mac the perfect excuse for calling Wilson, one of their junior repair guys, in early. He needed to see her now.

He hadn't seen Charlie since she left for college several years ago, but today looked like his lucky day. He was hopeful it would be the start of something good for he and Dillon.

He had heard through Charlie's Aunt Trudy that she had graduated from NYU's law school a year ago and was practicing in some swanky law firm in New York City. It was a blessing when Trudy would give them updates on how Charlie was doing in the big apple.

Knowing that Charlie's parents had recently been killed in a car crash, he knew it was the only reason she had come back to Crave.

Trying to make a mental picture in his head of what Charlie Maxwell looked like was not working for him. He did the next best thing, pulled out his iPhone and did a quick Google search. Typing in her name, he was amazed what appeared on the small screen. A beautiful woman's profile and a picture took up most of the screen. He recognized her instantly.

Our Charlie.

Her eyes still sparkled like emeralds, but they also told another story, they looked weary, lost, and even isolated.

Her face was made up with makeup but he could still see the dark circles under her eyes. A sweet smile rounded out her high cheekbones. Her hair still held a mass of unruly red curls; she almost looked like she had just been fucked sensibly.

Most men would see this picture and move on to something bigger and better looking, but not Mac; he saw something else in the photo. He saw a woman that looked lost; she had submissive written all over her face. He had seen that look in her eyes years ago and did nothing about it. He could kick himself in the ass for not acting on his impulses. Her striking curls framed around her neck gave even more erotic enticement.

Slowly panning down to her breasts, he could tell they had filled out nicely. *Fuck, wish they showed a full silhouette of her entire body. Would love to see her luscious hips. Such a tease not to see the entire woman.*

He wasn't about to waist another minute. He was going to pull out all of his Domly Dom-ness and charm the pants right off of Charlie Maxwell. First, he needed to get in touch with the other part of this trio, his brother Dillon.

Not even thinking he dialed his brother's cell, but to his dismay, it went straight to voicemail. Knowing that his brother had requested not to be disturbed while he was fishing, Mac did the next best thing. He sent a quick text.

MAC: Hey bro, I know you said not to bother you, but I found our missing puzzle piece.

Attaching the link about Charlie Maxwell, Mac hit the sent button.

It only took Dillon a few seconds to respond.

DILLON: What's up man, is she in trouble?

MAC: Broken air conditioner at the diner. But...I see something in her eyes that tells me she needs something else.

DILLON: US????

MAC: You read my mind Bro. How fast can you be at Maxwell's Diner?

DILLON: at the lake, 30 minutes tops.

MAC: meet you there

As soon as Mac read the last text, he had to get his shit together, that way when he walked into the diner, hopefully he would be setting sights on his new future.

Life was surely looking brighter in the eyes of Mackenzie Ryder; he set out for the biggest mission of his life, securing Charlotte "Charlie" Maxwell as theirs.

Growing up all of his life in the small town of Crave, Dillon Ryder was known as the quirky, mischievous prankster, who never got caught at doing anything wrong. Several times, he had broken into the chemistry lab of Sherwood High School. He'd take out their experiments and replace the test tubes with jello.

When his fellow classmates would arrive for class, they'd all think that their experiments had gone through some kind of scientific reaction and would need to be redone. That's how Dillon rolled. He was the local prankster.

He was a superstar on and off the football field. Every girl in Crave County wanted to be his girl, but he only had eyes for one, and she never had eyes for him or his brother.

Always trying to push himself to the fullest, he met his match one day on the football field and had to be carried off with a torn ACL. Ending his football career his senior year in high school, Dillon did his best to rebound by excelling at anything else he ever touched. Football was out of the picture and so was his full ride to UCLA. Instead, he and his brother decided to stick it out together and go to college in their hometown.

Crave University was not fancy like UCLA but an education was an education in their parents' eyes. The two boys had a tighter bond after Dillon's accident and grew closer than they had ever been.

Life was full of difficulties, but as he always said if something bad had to happen to them, he was glad it happened to him.

Getting the call from his brother snapped Dillon out of the funk that he'd been living in for the past six months. He'd come to a point in his life when playing with a submissive with his brother where the spark was no longer there.

Sex had become a rote chore, something he did because he had to do it. Something was missing. He was simply scratching an itch. He longed to find his lifelong submissive. No one had satisfied him yet. Maybe it was time for him to leave Crave and venture out on his own.

Dillon had been thinking about leaving for the past four months. He hadn't brought it up to his family yet, but he was constantly looking at his options. Leaving his brother to fend for himself, he felt like a lost star hovering up in the clouds.

Dillon was like most guys looking for his missing puzzle piece. What he wasn't sure about now was would it be with his brother or would he be searching alone.

It was startling to think about a life that didn't include sharing a woman with his brother. He would do it if they couldn't find the right fit with the two of them. His clock was definitely ticking. He had put an end of summer date of making his decision. That date was only a little over a month away.

Getting the text message about Charlie suddenly gave him a fresh gleam of hope. He'd always had a thing for her but she was so fucking untouchable. She was smart, strong, and only hung out with the brainy kids from school, whereas he and Mac hung out with the jocks.

Occasionally he did get a chance to run into her in the halls of school, but he never took the plunge to ask her out.

Now, after all these years, she had returned to their hometown, needing his help. Looking at her picture told Dillon that she was lost, alone, and submissive. Her eyes burned a whole in heart. She looked like a recluse.

Whether she looked like that now, the photo was burning a hole in his mind. He knew that the photo was dated over a year ago because it announced her law school graduation. Did she still have that same drawn look? He'd soon fine out.

Quickly he packed up all of his fishing equipment, realizing the sooner he got on the road the faster he could rescue his damsel in distress. Dillon didn't waist a single second. He rushed over to his Hummer, threw his fishing gear in the back, and high tailed it back to Crave.

The entire drive back he envisioned her tiny little hand wrapped around his shaft while she sucked his brother off. Suddenly he felt the spark that he had been missing just thinking about Charlie.

His cock twitched in his shorts telling him that he was returning to his old self. The dragon inside his soul had been awakened.

He wondered if she had ever been with two guys at once. Most girls from Crave had no problem with being surrounded by more than one man, but thinking back he never saw Charlie with any guy, let alone with more than two.

God his missing puzzle piece had been staring at him for so long. *How could I have been so blind and stupid not to see her for her beauty?* Charlie Maxwell, his little butterfly.

He wanted to fuck his little redhead until she couldn't walk the next day. His cocked hardened even more just thinking about being buried deep inside her. Even better, thoughts of having her tied up in a fancy Shibari suspension, he could fuck her while she sucked his brother's cock or vice versa.

If he kept these thoughts up, he'd blow his load in his shorts before he even got the chance to see her in person. He had to get a grip, before he made a complete fool of himself. He couldn't walk into Maxwell's with a hard on, or even worse, a big old wet spot on the front of his shorts.

Christ no he couldn't.

Control yourself man, you have plenty of time to win the girl of your dreams. He had better self-control then this. He was acting like a fucking teenager in heat.

CHAPTER 4

Pulling up to Maxwell's Diner, seeing an ambulance and a police car parked out front of the diner, sent a spark of panic throughout Mac's entire body. He had only talked to Charlie less than an hour ago.

He knew that the diner wasn't open for another hour or so. So why was there an ambulance and police car parked out front?

Stepping out of his Hummer, Mac walked briskly over to the entrance to the diner, where he was quickly met by a very upset, shaken Gloria.

"What's going on, sweetheart?" Luckily, for Mac, Gloria and he had been friends ever since the two were in diapers. He hadn't seen Gloria this upset since her brother had returned home from Iraq after being badly injured.

Gloria could normally handle just about anything that was forced upon her. Except seeing her friends suffer. So when Mac saw her face he immediately knew that someone was seriously wrong.

Taking Gloria's hand in his Mac simply stroked her knuckles trying to calm her down. "Tell me what's going on."

"I went over to Charlie to tell her that today's specials were all lined up in the kitchen, and the next thing I know she's got a dazed look on her face, her clothes are drenched in sweat, then all of a sudden, she's on the ground. Passed out cold. So I called Doc Owens to come over and look at her. And I had Greg call her Aunt Trudy. Mac she looked so bad I didn't know what was happening to her."

"Alright, Gloria, no need to get yourself all worked up, or Doc Owens will have two patients to deal with."

Mac kissed the top of Gloria's head giving her a little reassurance. Knowing that she was a true submissive to the core, Mac needed to have Gloria refocus not on Charlie but on something peaceful, because if she kept dwelling she would be no good for the rest of the day.

In his most stern Dom voice, Mac ordered Gloria to go sit on a bench in front of the diner. She was instructed to wait for Aunt Trudy. No one was allowed to enter the diner except for Aunt Trudy or Dillon.

"I'm going to go talk to Doc Owens to see if he needs another set of hands. Do you understand, Gloria?"

"Yes, Sir. I'll man the door."

"Good, sweetheart, if you need anything just peek your head through the door."

Mac pulled out his phone and sent a text to his brother.

MAC: problem Charlie passed out, what's your ETA?

DILLON: WTF...is she ok? 10 min

MAC: Don't know...Our girl needs us. Get your ass here.

Mac had to get his shit together before he walked into the diner, he wasn't sure what he was walking into, but he knew his mind was made up. He was going after Charlie Maxwell.

He saw a figure lying flat on the floor. Walking as fast as he could, his heart began to race in his chest. He knew that his girl was in need of help and this just proved to him that no matter what he would stand by her for the rest of his life.

Having not seen her in person for almost six years except for photos by god she was the most gorgeous women he had ever laid eyes on.

She was just as he'd remembered. Her perfect alabaster skin was still covered with freckles. Nice and curvy. Her long slender legs would wrap around his waist as she rode his cock. He had to gain control over his overacting libido before he ejaculated in his shorts.

He bent down next to his girl, who lay motionless on the floor. Doc had already placed an IV in her arm and had an oxygen mask placed over her mouth and nose. He could see that she was breathing; the only thing moving on her was the rise and fall of her luscious breasts.

"Doc, how's she doing?"

"I think she's just a little dehydrated and suffering from heat exhaustion that's all. A little rest and she'll be good as new."

Mac let out a sigh of relief. He placed his large hand around her tiny hand and held on for dear life. He could be her big, burly protector, as long as she was his.

Feeling her stir just a bit, he squeezed her hand. He watched as she slowly opened her calm, gentle loving eyes. He remembered how they were bright and round when the bright sun bounced off them. Her eyes sparkle like large pieces of jade. The kind you would see from China in the statues of the dragons.

Looking at her eyes was like looking through a mirror to her soul. He saw the weary look she now had plastered all over her face. It would be his and Dillon's job to get her back to the happy girl he once knew.

Slowly opening her eyes, Charlie saw the most gorgeous man kneeling beside her. She'd recognize him even if she had amnesia. Trying to figure out why she was laying on the floor at the diner with a man on her right that she didn't recognize and Mac on her left startled her.

Without hesitation Charlie began to sit up, but hearing Mac's voice to *lie still* she did as he commanded her to do. Still feeling like she was in some fairytale dream Charlie looked around the room some more and finally down to her right arm where she saw the IV protruding out of her arm. She mumbled, "What's going on?"

"I'm Doc Owens, Ms. Maxwell, you passed out, and Gloria called me to check up on you."

"How long have I been out?"

"Not long at all, maybe a few minutes. Lucky for you I was in the neighborhood when I got the call. Have you always had a low blood pressure or is this new?"

"Ever since high school, but my new physician back in New York treats me."

"Any other medical problems that I need to know about?"

She stuttered slightly before answering the good doctor's question. She felt her heart begin to pound, when her gaze met Dillon's as he strolled into the diner.

"Sweetie can you answer Doc's question he needs to know how to best treat you. Don't worry about a thing. Dillon and I are going to take care of you."

Panic struck her hard as she listen to the last words Mac had just said to her they were going to take care of her. She had longed to hear those words coming from a man's mouth, especially his, but deep down in her heart she feared he only said those words to soothe and comfort her.

It was a forbidden thing, thinking about the two of them in an erotic way. The moment she looked back up, she saw both of them glaring down at her. Dillon was now at her other side. As he bent down closer to her, she stared into his eyes; suddenly she saw the truth.

They both would take care of her.

"Hey you, I heard you were having a bad day" is what came out of the sexy, gorgeous, Dillon Ryder. She hadn't heard his voice in so long. It almost put her in a light trance.

"I've had better. How about you?"

"My day just got a whole lot brighter now that I know you're going to be okay. Now I think Doc Owens needs to know if you have any other health problems."

"I've been anemic in the past. I take a sleeping pill occasionally to fall asleep. That's about it."

"Ms. Maxwell, have you ever passed out before?" Charlotte shook her head signaling yes to Doc Owens.

"I'd like to take you over to County Hospital to run some tests that I can't do out in the field. That way we can be sure this was due to dehydration and not something going on with your heart to cause your blood pressure to drop."

This really wasn't what she wanted to hear. She started to protest when her Aunt Trudy came busting through the door.

"How's my girl doing?" The fiery redhead came to a sudden halt in front of everyone, her hands were waving around, and her mouth was spouting off words that were almost hard to understand.

No wonder Aunt Trudy was loved by everyone in the town. She could make a gloomy day turn bright with just the laughter raised deep down from her soul.

"I'm good, Aunt Trudy; I just decided that I needed a little attention from these three good looking guys. That's all"

All four of them looked down at Charlie and busted out laughing.

"Doc did you check her for a concussion? Did she hit her head when she passed out?"

"Why would you think that Trudy?"

"Because that's the funniest thing Charlie has said in months. She must be delusional."

"What? You don't think Charlie could use some attention from us guys?" Mac.

"Well I didn't quite say that, Mac. Seems to me that since Doc Owens is already spoken for that only leaves you two bozos giving my girl attention."

Aunt Trudy let that little smirk escape her mouth. Just as Charlie let out a giggle. She felt like everyone was staring at her. If the floor would just swallow her up she could easily get out of her little slip of the tongue.

She had to think before she said anything else, because she wasn't sure if it was really a slip of the tongue, or if she really wanted the Ryder brothers to take care of her.

"So what's the plan, Doc? I saw the ambo outside. Are you taking her to County?"

"That's what we were discussing when you came in, Aunt Trudy. I think I'm going to be just fine, but Doc here wants to run some test to make sure this was just a fluke."

She felt two set of hands on her at once. It sent little shivers up and down her spine. For the first time in a long time, she actually felt something. She wasn't sure what she was feeling but she surely did like it.

"We agree with Doc, Charlie. You need to go and get checked out." Dillon said.

"Don't worry about a thing. Dillon and I will stay here at the diner; it will give us a chance to check the air compressor out while you and Aunt Trudy go to the hospital.

When were done we'll come over and check on you. How's that sound sweetie?"

"I guess if my choices are stay here and sweat to death, or go to a nice air conditioned hospital. Well that's a no brainer."

"Good. Your chariot awaits you ma'am."

Slowly Dillon put his arm under her back and her knees he gingerly picked her up and placed her curvy body on the gurney that had been brought in by the paramedics.

Looking around the room, Charlie searched for the one person that she must have scared the crap out of, but with all of the chaos, she didn't see the woman she was looking for. "Where's Gloria? I might have frightened her."

"She's sitting outside on the bench. I gave her an order to stay there until I knew what was going on."

"Did you take on sweet Gloria as your sub?" Aunt Trudy burst out.

"No as a matter of fact we have our eyes set on someone, but she doesn't quite know it yet."

"Can you get her for me please? I need to make sure she's okay."

"You got it, babe."

Dillon got even closer to her like he was her protector and nothing was going to come between the two of them. She actually felt special that a guy she once knew would be so protective over her since they hadn't seen each other in so long. She wasn't going to complain. In a way, she really liked it a lot.

Finally, someone to look after me. Or was she just thinking with her heart and not her brain?

After talking with Gloria and calming her down, Charlie gave specific instructions to her about making sure all the menus for today were to be updated on the bulletin boards and if for some strange reason Charlie wasn't able to close up tonight, Gloria was to have Greg stay with her.

He normally stayed with Charlie while she was tinkering about after everyone left anyway, but secretly she knew Greg had a thing for Gloria and that's why he stuck around.

Giving the two Ryder brothers last minute instructions on the broken air compressor had been just Charlie spouting out words. She was sure neither brother paid attention to anything she actually said.

She was up front with both of them about how much she could afford. Both brothers just shook their heads and told her not to worry her silly head over the repairs.

She had to worry though because she only had a little bit of her parents' inheritance left and it had to go a long ways to getting Maxwell's Diner up for sale or keeping as her own.

Charlie still wasn't sure which she was going to do yet, but she knew that her clock was ticking. She had to make a decision about returning to her position back in New York. The firm had already warned her that if she didn't come to a decision soon, they were going to let her go.

Asking for an extension on her bereavement leave was something that bought her only another month. Speaking to her boss weekly, he constantly told her she had until August 1st. The clock was ticking down and fast.

She wouldn't worry about that today; instead, she had to make sure her passing out spell was just that and nothing more.

CHAPTER 5

Three hours later, Charlie felt like a human pincushion. She had been poked, prodded, x-rayed, fluffed, and tucked. All she wanted to do now was go back to her parents' house, crawl into bed, and sleep for at least a week. We'll maybe not a week, but at least until tomorrow.

If she hadn't been tired before coming to the hospital, she was completely exhausted now. Her aunt had stayed with her all day, even she looked exhausted, and nothing made that bubbling woman look tired. She was like the energizer bunny; she kept going and going. Now she looked like her batteries needed to be replaced.

Catching a few small little cat naps in-between tests were all Charlie had been able to get. Still no Doc Owens to tell her what was going on which started to worry Charlie just a bit.

What if something is really wrong with me? Who would take care of me? I can't expect my Aunt to do it all on her own.

Just as she was thinking those horrible thoughts, two beautiful hunks walked into her room. She buried those feelings; she didn't need them worrying about her too.

One thing was for sure when these two guys walked into the room they brightened up her day. Both filled up the doorway with their large, chiseled bodies blocking out all light coming from the hallway.

Mac was carrying a bouquet of flowers and Dillon had two balloons tied to his wrist. Aunt Trudy jumped when she saw them walking in. She had been slumped over in a chair fast asleep.

"Look what the cat dragged in."

"Nice to see you too, Aunt Trudy."

"Well, boys, you really shouldn't have gone through all the trouble of bringing me flowers and balloons."

Shocked at how her aunt was talking to the Ryder twins, Charlie just shook her head.

"These happen to be for Charlie. I believe you got flowers from us a few months ago when it was your birthday."

She watched as her aunt had her fun with these two guys. They all did get along nicely, which didn't surprise her at all because everyone loved her Aunt Trudy.

Turning their attention away from her aunt, both men focused on her as if she was some kind of prey. She saw them as her hungry lions and she being their lioness. Both men had eyes as bright as the deep blue sea and a look of desire written all over their faces.

Could she put her past in the past and maybe follow her heart for a change? Could they hold the key to her happiness?

How would she really know if they were interested in her, for her, and not a quick romp in the hay? She had heard so many stories of guys using and losing women just like old socks. She didn't want to be part of that statistic. She needed to look towards her future and she still didn't know what that held for her. Yet.

"How's our number one patient doing?" Both guys walked over and sat down on each side of the bed. Charlie felt like she was being surrounded by testosterone. If she hadn't been diagnosed with having a stroke earlier then she was sure she was going to have one now.

"I'm off for some coffee. You two guys want a cup?" Aunt Trudy yelled as she made her way to the door.

Both guys replied in unison. "Black, two sugars.

"You two are really twins through and through." Charlie giggled. "We'll I've been poked, prodded, x-rayed, cat scanned, and still no Doc Owens to tell me what's wrong. I guess no news is good news right?"

"That's the perfect attitude to take, Charlie, but really how are you feeling darling?" Mac.

Charlie saw something at that very moment she had never seen with any other guy before. Mac had a deep look of concern and so did Dillon. These guys really cared about her.

She felt tears start to roll down her cheeks. She didn't know exactly why she was crying but she knew she needed to. She felt the hospital bed shift as both guys at the same time put their arms around her. Feeling the warmth coming from their bodies sent her mind, body, and soul into a frenzy. It was the first time in years that she actually felt something besides anger, sorrow, or even disgust at a man's touch.

Now she was being touched by two men and she didn't feel like her skin was being burned with acid. Instead, she felt a calm, peaceful existence between the three of them.

"Charlie, what's the matter? Did Doc give you bad news? Whatever it is, Mac and I are here for you."

She had to tell them that it had nothing to do with her health, but deep down inside she didn't want to let go of either one of them.

Before she could say a thing, Dillon pulled a tissue from the side table. She felt him gingerly began wiping her tears away. "Now, beautiful girl, are you going to tell us what the matter is?"

"I just, well..." Charlie started to fidget in the bed. She wasn't sure how to tell them that she might be having feeling towards the two of them.

So she stuffed that part down. Without even thinking, she blurted out how she was just exhausted from dealing with her parents affairs. She went on and on about the diner, the house, until she was sobbing again and cradled in their arms.

She even told them about how she was under a deadline with work to make a decision in the next month or she would lose her position at the law firm. Nothing seemed to bother either of the Ryder twins as Charlie let her heart bleed out about all of her fears.

Mac and Ryder shared something that most twins shared. They could fell what the other twin was feeling without even letting the other twin know. If one was sick, the other could sense it.

Same way if they got hurt the other could at the exact time feel the pain hurting the other twin. Both felt the pain Charlie had been enduring for the past months. Both guys hated seeing her in such agony and distress.

They saw the pain in her eyes, and felt it deep down in their souls. She needed them. Neither was going to stand by and watch Charlie leave Crave. They would do their damnedest to keep her here forever. Just as they had settled Charlie down, Doc Owens knocked on the door.

As he entered, he was holding a few x-rays and several pieces of paper. Neither Mac nor Dillon budged a bit when Doc Owens approached Charlie. They felt Charlie tense under both of their arms when she saw all the stuff Doc was carrying.

"So, am I going to die?" Charlie squeaked.

"Not on my watch, but we do need to discuss some minor issues that showed up in your blood results. Your blood counts are low, indicating you're anemic again, and your blood sugar is low also."

Charlie tensed even more. Though she was in the arms of her two protectors, she still felt like she was alone. She was surprised that both guys stroked her shoulders trying to soothe her.

It seemed to work too as each one went up and down her arms she let out the slightest moan indicating she was enjoying their special attention.

"I'm guessing you already know the next question out of my mouth is going to be. Don't you, Charlie?" Charlie needed to run, hide, anything to get out of this situation.

She just wanted to pull the covers over her head and pretend that no one was in the room except for her, but she really didn't think the two hunks that were sitting in her bed would let her just hide. So instead she knew the time to face her fears where starring her in the face. It was time to face the music.

CHAPTER 6

She felt like she had been just kicked by a horse in her gut. Most likely, all of her secrets that she held locked up would need to be told. She looked at both men sitting by her side she didn't want to lose them, but she wasn't ready to share her secrets just yet.

"What's Doc Owens talking about, Charlie?"

She grabbed both of their hands at the same time. "I really appreciate everything that both of you have done for me today. I hope you left a bill with Gloria. I'll be sure to get you a check by the end of the week."

"What the fuck are you talking about a bill for, Charlie? The money means nothing to Dillon and me. We care about you and your well-being."

Both men seemed to be crowding her on the small hospital bed. She knew she had pissed them off by trying pushing them away. Charlie immediately shut down all of her emotions. She put on her stern courtroom face, the one she had worn for the past eight years since being raped by Carl Hughes.

"I need to talk to you, Doctor Owens, in private please." She watched as three sets of eyes now stared at her. They could have burned a hole into her as hard as they were staring at her.

"As my doctor, I know you'll honor the patient to doctor privilege of not sharing my medical findings."

"Ms. Maxwell, I assure you I will do whatever you, as the patient, wants. Gentlemen, I think Ms. Maxwell is trying to ask you politely to leave us to discuss her medical problems."

Charlie felt the temperature in the room go up by at least ten degrees. Both guys were now steamy mad. She had to protect herself from both of them. She needed to sell the diner and move back to New York as soon as possible.

Her mind was made up. As soon as she was released from the hospital, she would tell her aunt of her plans, get back in touch with the realtor, and be back in New York by the beginning of next week. *Oh, Fuck. The Fourth of July event is tomorrow, I'll just tell everyone on the fifth.*

She watched as both men became extremely pissed, giving a harsh stare at Doc Owens.

"If you were ours, Charlie, we would have no secrets between the three of us."

She couldn't fully register what Mac was saying to her because she felt like she was going to be sick again. Both turned and told her that they would wait outside until her and the Doc talked about her medical history. She couldn't bear to see them anymore, she was already feeling like she had just had her heart ripped out, or worse she had just ripped their hearts out.

"Guys go ahead and go. Aunt Trudy will be back in a few minutes. I'll be just fine until she returns."

Both men in a very stern, brash voice said no at the said time. She knew she had triggered their over protectiveness. Neither guy was willing to walk away without a huge fight, nor didn't she just have it in her to fight the two of them.

"We'll wait outside in the hall until Aunt Trudy gets back with our coffee. By then you should be finished with doc here, and then well discuss this together. No, ifs, ands, or buts. We're not ready for you to kick us to the curbs, so to speak."

"You nearly tore my heart out when I saw you laying out on the diner floor this morning," Mac said to her as he squeezed her hand. Let us take care of you, in the manner you should be. Sometimes it better to face your fears with people by your side instead of by yourself. I can see that written all over your face, I saw it when I googled you this morning. Your picture says a thousand words and none of its good. The darkness is written all across your face."

God how could these two guys be so damn pushy, and so right at the same time. They weren't go to take no for an answer.

"I need to talk to doc by myself. Please just give me that."

"A good Dom never leaves a submissive in distress. You, my dear, are a damsel in distress. We aim to rescue you. Dillon and I will be just out there."

"What makes the two of you think I'm a submissive by the way?"

"Because you are, Charlie. I bet if you ask Doc Owens the same question, he would say the same thing. Am I right Doc?"

"Through and through, Ms. Maxwell, but at this very moment your health is what concerns me." Doc turned to both of the men. "I need to talk to Ms. Maxwell. I want you two to give us a few minutes, and then if Ms. Maxwell wants you guys I'll come and get you."

"You got it, Doc, we'll be outside. Take all the time in the world, Charlie. We're not going anywhere."

She watched as her two men walked to the door. *No, they aren't my men.* She wasn't sure why she felt so horrible for not wanting them to hear what Doc had to say to her, she just wasn't ready to share her secrets yet.

As the heard the door shut behind them, she let out a sigh. Tears rolled down the sides of her cheeks. All she thought about was how she had finally had them in her life, suddenly she knew that it wasn't going to last.

She ran her hand over the top of the sheet that warmed her body now. It was her security blanket, since she didn't have her own little blanket her mother made for her when she was a baby. Unfortunately, it was back at the diner sitting in her purse.

Charlie never went anywhere without it.

Not wanting to stall anymore, it was best if she just broke the silence between her and the good doctor. "So how bad's my blood count?"

"It pretty low, Ms. Maxwell."

"Please, Doc, just call me Charlie like everyone else. My mother was Ms. Maxwell, I'm known by everyone as Charlie."

"Alright then, Charlie, your hemoglobin is ten and your crit is thirty five. When's the last time you ate a healthy meal?" She was feeling so busted. When things got rough in her life, she'd stop eating. This had started after being raped. She became so distracted about her issues, she neglected herself with nutrients.

Receiving counseling for many years she thought she had learned to control her eating disorder, but when she returned back home three months ago, she hadn't received any counseling in Crave, even though her counselor back in New York had suggested that she seek services from her old counselor, so that she didn't have a trigger that set her off.

She didn't take his advice. She did the total opposite, she worked herself every day and night to complete exhaustion, forgetting to eat and get a proper night's sleep. She was now back in the same old scenario that burdened her so many times before. She had let her fears and stress win this round.

"I placed a call to your doctor back in New York, Charlie; he was very helpful in sending me your medical records. We had a nice long chat about your eating disorder, your panic attacks, and I know about your being raped. I've reviewed everything in your file."

Charlie started to squirm in the bed, knowing that everything that Doc Owens said was true, she had nowhere to run, hide, or escape.

She had to face what he was going to say to her just like her other doctors; she knew that they only wanted to see Charlie happy and healthy. Tears burned her eyes as she let her emotions get the best of her.

"Lucky for you, I think you now have two things looking up for you. Well maybe three. One...the death of your parents had to come as a huge shock to you. You're not alone, and your Aunt Trudy is willing to help you in any way possible. I know for a fact that if you let her she would be willing to help you run the diner, while you figure out what you want to do with it.

Secondly, the two men that are standing outside the door only have your best intentions in mind. I've known them since I moved to town a few years ago, and I can tell you, that all three of you would be perfect for each other. They like taking charge of situations and handling problems. They already see you as theirs, Charlie. If you could have seen the look on Mac's face when he saw you lying on the floor earlier you...well just say I've never seen him look that way over a beautiful woman before.

I've seen the two of them often at The Farm many times with other submissives, but I've never seen the two of them as happy as I have today. It's like you've been missing from their lives all these years and now that your back, well I see the joy in all of your faces."

She listened to Doc's words. She heard what he was saying but never realized the severity of his words until his last statement, that the Ryder twins had been lost for several years too.

Something shifted inside her heart as she let his words sink in. They needed her. Just as much as she needed them.

"Lastly, we need to get you back up on your feet because tomorrow is the Fourth of July picnic. What kind of picnic would it be without the famous Maxwell's Diner being able to feed all of the great citizens of Crave? If I don't get their fearless leader out of the hospital, I might get lynched."

"We can't have that now. You're the only doctor in town, right?"

"For the time being, I'm your guy. Before I release you, I took the liberty in calling Lisa Phillips. She's going to come by and talk to you; I think you'll remember her. She might have been a few years ahead of you in school.

She's very familiar with counseling people that have been raped, not just women but also men. She also can answer any questions that you might have about dealing with those two beefcake guys. Lucky for you she is a submissive she can give you pointers and insight into our kinky world.

Plus, it is good to be able to talk to another submissive that has learned many tricks of the trade. She is also well connected in the community.

I'm going to have the nurse come in and give you an iron infusion. That should give you and Lisa Phillips some time to talk over some of your issues. After getting the infusion, you should notice you'll have a burst of energy to burn off. Do you have any questions for me?"

"No I think you've laid out everything for me. I know what I must do."

"What's that, Charlie?"

"I've got to learn how to trust others, and I know that I'm going to need a lot of help and guidance, and patience. I'm just hoping I'm going to survive this."

"You just gave me the best answer that anyone could have given. You said you needed to trust, that would mean a lot. When you finally feel comfortable, trust me when I say those two guys are what you're missing. With that being said I'm going to go and take your two Neanderthals out for a cup of coffee that your Aunt Trudy promised them an hour ago."

"How did you know that?"

"She met me in the hall when I was about to talk to you. Instead we, let's just say we got side tracked."

Charlie's face was now as red as a ripe summer tomatoes. "But I thought you were happily married?

"I am. That doesn't mean a Dom can't have more than one wife in Crave County. Does it Charlie?"

"Oh, my god she never even said a thing to me. I would have never guessed she would remarry after what her first husband did to her. I have been so caught up with my problems that I never noticed that she was finally happy. I feel like such as horrible niece."

Charlie gave the doctor a contemplative stare.

"See, Charlie, everyone can change. Your aunt has found a way to be happy. I believe you can too. We haven't made anything official yet. We were hoping to do that tomorrow at the cookout. June is so excited that Trudy will finally be joining our family. She's even at home cooking up something special for our family's contribution to the festivities.

I'm hoping now that my new niece, who happens to be a terrific lawyer, will be able to draw up a new will for the Owens family."

Doc gave her a smirk that told her he knew more than what he was going to tell her. "Don't worry, Charlie. I already talked to the other board members we all know that your license is good for Crave County. I understand running the diner is not what you want to be doing full time. Lucky for you, your family made sure that anytime you wanted to come home and practice law you would have no trouble with hanging your shingle.

So think about everything that I've just told you. Consider being a part of my family. Your fathers kept after me for two years to make an honest woman out of Trudy. Tears flowed down Charlie's cheeks as she listened to her soon to be uncle explain to her how he loved her aunt.

"I just wished I would have stepped up sooner. Trudy and your mom would have loved celebrating with us tomorrow, but now instead we get to celebrate it with you." As she let his words settle, he kissed the top of her head and headed out the door.

CHAPTER 7

After receiving the iron infusion and an hour-long conversation with Lisa Phillips, Charlie knew not all of her problems were solved but she had another way of looking at her future. She had to come to grips with what had happened to her and move on. It was going to take her time do this but she now had access to tools that she didn't before.

Lisa had given her a list of support groups for people who had been raped. She felt this was the best way for Charlie to see that she wasn't the only person in the world that felt damaged.

Charlie had used the word damaged about fifty times before Lisa had actually stopped her and said she needed to not talk about herself as damaged but instead she needed to think of ways to make her feel special again.

Lisa gave her some suggestions the one that stuck in her head was she needed to reconnect with her friends. She had constantly put them off when they called for get-togethers. One excuse after another always played at the tip of Charlie's tongue when someone called, or she's just wouldn't answer the calls. She'd be doing no more of that in the future.

She could think back to just last week when her friend Justine came into the diner and asked if Charlie would like to go and have a spa day. She'd made every excuse under the sun on why she couldn't spend time with her friend.

Shit even Gloria had even asked if they could go to the movies or even get a movie and watch it with a big bucket of popcorn and wine. Charlie said no that she had so much to do at the house that she couldn't spare the time.

Looking back at her last three months in Crave, she blew just about everyone off. She hadn't had girl time in forever. She kept to herself and liked being alone.

Well of course, she didn't, but it was better to pretend that she did, that way she could feel sorry for herself. Then the vicious circle would start, she wouldn't eat, couldn't sleep which lead up to where she was today. Stuck in a hospital room with a tube in her arm giving her liquid strength. She didn't want to depend on liquid strength anymore, she need to be around friends, especially the new family that would be announced tomorrow.

She even let Lisa know about her feelings for the Ryder twins. She wasn't sure how they would handle knowing that one of their friends had raped her. Or that she'd had no physical contact with a man since being raped.

Would they accept her as she was? Or would they walk away, not wanting to get involved with a person dealing with a disease? Eating disorders had been classified as a disease in the medical community many years ago, but Charlie never believed that she had such an issue until after almost dying a couple years back.

Lucky for her she didn't have to worry her parents, she just told them she had a serious stomach bug and that her doctors in New York felt it better to be treated as an inpatient in the hospital.

She had finally convinced her Aunt Trudy that she didn't need her parents coming to New York to take care of her. She never told her aunt the truth. She needed to come clean with a lot of stuff that she held locked away.

She'd start out by first telling her aunt about her past medical issues over the past few years. She was most sure that her aunt would stand by her side but she needed to be honest with her.

Secondly, she'd need some help with the diner. She knew the diner held a special place in everyone's heart especially for her Aunt Trudy. She was the closest person that she had in her life at this moment in time.

The closeness that her mom and aunt had was a special bond. Charlie wished her parents had given her a sister for her to share all of her secrets with.

THEIRS TO LOVE

Maybe asking for help with updating the place could take some of the burden off her plate. Moreover, she could use another woman's opinion in decorating. Since Charlie wasn't actually a New York fashion expert, her aunt did have the eye for just that.

The way Trudy dressed was a testimony just to that. The latest and greatest fashion hung in a small boutique that Trudy ran. She could sparse up the look of the diner.

Charlie needed a girl's night out to be with other females. It would bring her out of the loneliness that she felt. She needed to hear the local gossip and she didn't need to hear it just from her aunt. She needed to be part of the inner circle she once had been a part of back in high school. She loved it when the girls got together. Now, they would most likely be talking about, husbands, babies, or what to cook for dinner. That was okay with Charlie; she just wanted to belong again.

Lastly, she had known for years that she was a true heart submissive. She had done some research back a few years ago when she started to go back in the dating world. One of her friends in at the law firm got a few of the girls together for a night out to a dungeon 101 class.

Charlie did the research and found out a lot of stuff about being kinky; she already came from a very kinky upbringing by growing up in Crave.

She had no problems doing things for others, but she never did them for herself. She actually liked being told what to do, how to do it, and when to do it. She had no problems taking orders from others. These are all characteristic of a submissive.

Hearing Doc say earlier today that he could tell that she was a submissive just confirmed her inner thoughts all along. She had never been in a serious relationship, nor have she even practiced anything that she had researched or seen at the dungeon.

Knowing that both Mac and Dillon were both dominants, she wasn't sure how they would react to her being a novice. Would they be open to helping her learn the ropes or would they be bored with her lack of trust?

She wouldn't know until they came back from having coffee. She had a taste of submission, but just wasn't sure how to use it yet. Both men were very powerful, strong, and bold. She even expected they were the same way in the bedroom.

Feeling both of their hands on her at the same time just about sent her into a frenzy. Every nerve ending in her upper arms had come to life just by them stroking her. She could only imagine what they would do to her once they had her in the bedroom. Excitement began to brew deep down in her soul something that had been dormant for a long time.

Charlie felt like a huge weight had been lifted from her shoulders today. For the first time in a long time, she actually felt like she meant something to both of the twins.

She hoped that she could love both of them at the same time. Deep down in her heart she had always secretly loved both of them, but never had she ever expressed her feelings for either one of them.

It had been so long since she merely just existed in body and not in her soul. She hoped that she could be what Mac and Dillon had been missing in their lives. She was their missing puzzle piece. Just now felt it more than what she had before. She hoped they felt it to.

She had dreamt about this so many times, but she never had the happy ending that every girl wished and hoped for, she had so many ghosts that filled her dreams. She wasn't sure she could sweep all her demons away. All she could do was to try to forge forward.

Seeing both of their bright faces as they entered the room brought the biggest smile to her face. She felt her heart burn with desire and her cheeks flush from the extra blood that was swirling around in her face. They must have noticed because both of them came to her at once.

"You, look so much better than few hours ago. What did they do to you?"

Secretly she knew that they would ask about her medical issues. She didn't want to go into everything with them all at once, and especially not in a hospital room. Therefore, instead of bringing down the mood, Charlie felt it was better to shed as little light on the subject as possible.

"I had to get an iron infusion to help out my anemia. It gave me a boost of energy as well. I feel well just say... Like I could run a marathon."

"That good hmm?" came from Dillon's sexy mouth.

"When can you be sprung from this joint baby?" She looked over at Mac who was now sitting on the edge of the bed reaching for her hand.

"I think as soon as the nurse comes back with my discharge instructions. Aunt Trudy hasn't been back since she left for her coffee break over three hours ago. I hope she's alright."

Both guys said at the same time, "she's perfectly fine."

"Oh she is, is she?" She was very fortunate that both men seemed to be in a better mood them when she last saw them.

Sending them on their way was one of the hardest things Charlie had ever done in her life. Now that she was being given a second chance, she was going to jump in the pool, feet first so to speak. She wasn't going to let these two big fishes get away. Not if she could help it.

Just as Dillon made his way over to the other side of her bed, a bubbly nurse came bouncing in with a stack of papers in her hand.

After completely going over line by line, Charlie's patience grew less and less as the time ticked on the clock. She had never seen someone as thorough as this nurse. She only wanted to be out of this place and back home, curled up on her sofa, suddenly Charlie remembered, "Oh shit. I need to go back to the diner to help back up everything for tomorrow. Can one of you guys give a stranded girl a ride, please?" She watched as both of them just shook their heads.

"No, were taking you home to your parents' house. So that you can rest up for the night..."

Before either one of them could get another word out of their mouths, Charlie said, "But, Mac. I need to go back and make sure everything is alright."

Charlie wasn't sure if they knew what a big deal the whole Fourth of July picnic meant to her and her family. She sure wasn't going to have her family's reputation under scrutiny.

"Baby, everything has been taken care of, that's why your aunt is not here now. Our job is to get you home safely, feed you, and then put you to bed."

All Charlie heard was his last statement of putting her to bed, which sent shivers up and down her spin. "Are you sure?"

"We are. Now go get your clothes on, so we can do what we said, home, eat, and sleep."

As she heard his voice echo throughout the room, her excitement rose up another notch. Why was she so thrilled by just the tone he had used on her. It was just mere words. Still it did something to her inner girl parts, she wasn't about to argue with either one of them.

Never in her wildest dreams did she ever imagine, sitting in the front seat of Mackenzie Ryder's Hummer, sandwiched between Mac and Dillon. She pinched the underside of her thigh just to make sure she wasn't actually dreaming.

No. She was wide awake.

During the drive, each guy took extra special care that she was fully comfortable. She could have been floating on cloud nine for all she knew. They both made her feel safe.

One minute she was wide awake watching out the window as they drove through the town of Crave, the next minute she had snuggled up to Dillon and was now fast asleep.

It must have been from the warmth of his body, because he didn't protest at all when she snuggled in even closer under his arm. She was using him like a big comfy pillow.

Gingerly, she felt a large pair of hands pick her up, opening her eyes slightly to see which guy was carrying her, and she saw that it was Mac. She was thankful that her aunt had stopped by the house and unlocked the front door for them, because she realized her purse was probably still at the diner.

Mac loved the feeling of this woman in his arms. She was as light as a feather. His job now was to see to her and her well-being. He needed to concentrate on getting her fattened up.

She was nothing but stick and bones in his mind. Yeah she had some curves to her hips. She needed some extra cushion for the pushing that he loved to give a woman. It truly felt amazing to Mac how she snuggled into his arms; she was a perfect fit for them.

He just hoped she felt the same way when she woke up.

Once Mac settled Charlie on the big leather sofa situated in the middle of the living room, Dillon handed him a large colorful patch quilt that he knew Charlotte's mother had made many years. Placing the quilt around her body, he tucked her in like a baby. Mac loved that she didn't object to him touching her in such an intimate way.

He could feel his cock thickening in his trousers; he had to will his mind to think about something else besides taking Charlie up to her bedroom and fucking her brains out. No, he had to be more civilized then that.

He watched as she dozed back off to dream land. She looked like an angel that had finally found peace. Her face now showed the lines that were once riddled with deep emotions that she buried deep down in her soul.

Her pale complexion that was once bright in her youth now stuck out as Mac stared at her majestic features. He and Dillon had to win her over and bring back that hidden beauty that she once has worn.

Thinking of all the ways that he could do just that brought back the memory of all of them going skinny-dipping. Maybe they could convince her to slip away tomorrow evening just before the fireworks to take a dip.

He watched as Dillon came back from the kitchen with a tray full of goodies. He'd give that to his brother; he was a wiz in the kitchen. He could make a six course meal out of well-stocked pantry. Looking at the tray, he could tell his brother had found enough for the three of them tonight.

"Did you make anything good?" Mac said softly to his brother not wanting to disturb their sleeping beauty.

"We need to either stock her pantry or take her to our house."

"I was wondering what was taking you so long in there. That bad hum?" Watching his brother set the tray down on the coffee table. Dillon made his way over to the love seat.

"You wouldn't believe that for a girl who inherited everything about her mother, the one thing Charlie didn't inherit was her mother's good cooking skills. Because by the looks of that kitchen, Charlie hasn't stepped foot in to make a complete meal yet. I think the only thing she uses is the microwave to heat up water for tea."

"I wonder why that is, Dillon?"

"Don't have a clue but that another question will need to ask her once she is feeling better."

"Let's not push her to hard. It just might scare her away.

"Yeah I was thinking that too. She does look beautiful all curled up on the sofa. She looked even better when she was curled up against you on the ride from the hospital.

It's the first time that I actually felt warmth from another woman. I don't know why that is but it's something that I can't explain. I know just how you're feeling, Dil. I felt it when we were holding her. She just melted into my side.

You remember how old Lucy the barn cat used to purr at our feet when she wanted our attention. Charlie reminds me of her. She's purring for our attention but just doesn't know how to say what she really wants."

"You're probably right man. We just need to figure out what's eating at Charlie's soul and once we do we just might have a chance at making her ours."

After watching their girl sleep for what seemed like forever? Both guys made a pledge to each other that they would do just about anything to make Charlie theirs. Neither one was willing to give up on her without a huge fight.

Seeing her stir awake had both of their hearts pounding in their chests. Not long after watching her eat everything that Dillon had prepared for them. Mac knew that he had to break the ice about bringing up tomorrow festivities.

Watching her intently both guys walked towards the sofa that Charlie had sprawled her long legs on the sofa.

Gently Mac picked her and the blanket that was snuggly wrapped around her body. Positioning himself on the sofa, placing her back on his lap, flanking the other side of the sofa he watched as Dillon sat down on the opposite side of the sofa.

Gently Dillon lifted up Charlie's feet placing them on top of his thighs. Just inches away from his throbbing dick. Never in his wildest dreams did either one of them ever think they would have a chance with Charlie, tonight hopefully they would push one step forward in the direction.

Gently stroking her upper arms while Dillon rubbed her feet and brought life back into her throbbing muscles. They felt Charlie stir about, watching her slowly wake up.

"Hey, Angel, we can't let you sleep the rest of the night away. We need to feed you, like we promised Doc Owens or he's going to come over here and take our Dom cards from us."

"Or better yet, your Aunt Trudy might beat the crap out of both Mac and I for not keeping to our promise of taking care of you properly."

Both guys felt Charlie snuggle into them even more. "I don't need to eat just yet. I'm so comfortable. Just laying here with you guys holding me is all I need or want at this minute."

Mac reached down and hugged her closer to his chest. He could fell her warmth radiating off her body onto his. Or was it his body giving off the heat from having his little kitten in his lap?

As Charlie got more comfortable, Dillon handed Mac half of a peanut butter and jelly sandwich. "Open up and I will feed you, kitten, since you're not willing to feed yourself.

For the first time ever, Charlie felt the weight she's been carrying around for years suddenly lifted. She felt secure, loved, and most importantly, she felt comfortable with the two guys holding her. She did the next best thing, she surrender to their wishes.

She opened her mouth and felt Mac place the sandwich in her mouth. She closed her eyes as she took her first step in healing. She needed the nutrition to help her gather up her strength. As she swallowed the morsels down her throat, tears formed in her eyes.

She became overwhelmed with emotions. "Kitten, why are you crying?" "I'm just feeling like this is a great dream that I happen to be in."

"Well I can tell you that you're not dreaming." She felt Dillon rubbing her feet, which just sent her mind into overdrive. This is how we treat our woman.

As a Dom, it's our job to see to your every existence. You're not to worry about a thing. Let Mac and I take all your cares off your shoulders."

"What if I can live up to your expectations? What if I'm I can't satisfy both of you. I can barely take care of myself."

"First off, you've been in our dreams ever since high school. Secondly, let us worry about satisfying you. We'll let you worry about satisfying us as time goes on." Hearing his words hit deep down in her heart. She never had anyone speak to her with such poise in his voice. Surprisingly to her she felt dampness covering her panties.

How could she be turned on just by his words? She shook her head in disbelief.

"Lastly, you can take care of yourself, you choose not to. Your priorities are just a little out of place. That's all. Look at you. You're sexy as all get out, smart, bold, courageous, strong lawyer, who has been on her own for several years."

She just listened to every word that rolled from his lips.

CHAPTER 8

She wondered what his lips would feel like on her entire body. Yep she was being turned on. Something that she hadn't experienced in a long ass time. Charlie sat cradled in Mac's arms, which felt so good.

"Now that we have that out in the open. You've heard Dillon and I say that we are both dominants correct?"

"Yes."

"And you're a submissive with no experience at letting others care for you. Is this also correct?" Mac said in his baritone voice.

"Yes."

"I'm so proud that you answered my questions without any hesitation. Everything that we do together is geared towards a D/s relationship." This is where Charlie began to get nervous. She remembered reading different articles on a site called Fetlife that explained about different kinky relationships. It had been only a little over a year since she visited the dungeon in New York. She was sure things couldn't have changed that much.

Sitting on Macs lap, while talking about sex was proving to be more difficult then she first thought. With Dillon continuously rubbing her feet, during their conversation, it drove her sexual desires even higher. She felt like she did back when she was a teenager with raging hormones.

She'd be a hot mess by the time these two would be done with her. But she already knew this is where she put a halt to everything. She was going to be in a sticky situation if she didn't speak up soon, but instead she just sat on Mac's lap as if she was in some kind of trance. All she knew was she needed to run, hide, or do anything to get herself out of this mess with Mac, and Dillon.

Somehow, she already knew neither one of them was going to let her go that easy. For some reason she wanted to be where she was, in between two hunky guys. *I want to be with them.* Is all she kept thinking?

Her body was turned on sexually, her mind was playing tricks on her, and now she couldn't even force her legs to move. So instead, she just sat there, aroused, listening to every word spoken to her.

"Charlie, have you been listening to a word I've said in the past five minutes?"

"Do you want an honest answer?"

She wasn't sure if it was his seductive voice that made her heart beat faster, or the constant erotic touching from Dillon, but whatever it was, they were playing havoc with her ability to even process words.

"Honesty is the number one rule in a D/s relationship. Her gaze kept darting back and forth between the two men. Both seemed to be intently staring at her with the eyes of a tiger. Ready to pounce her at any given second. As her heart began to race, she felt tiny beads of perspiration forming on her forehead. *How can I be so turned on by the sound of Mac's voice?*

If fate were on her side, she'd be able to listen to the rules of starting a D/s relationship with these two guys, but they would quickly realize that she had no experience and they'd both move on. But something told her they would be able to take on the challenge of shaping her into a well-rounded submissive.

Thoughts flickered through her mind. She pictured herself, kneeling naked with both of her men standing above her side by side, licking and sucking their cocks at the same time. The more she thought about fulfilling her sexual fantasies, the more she was turned on. Already her stomach clinched inside, as she twisted her hands together.

Trying to stop herself from thinking about her sexual desires, she let her mind wonder back to the diner. Was she going to keep it and run it, because of her parents' wishes or was she going to get the hell out of dodge, back to New York to her law career, or was she going to stay in Crave County and take on a the law position here and run the diner at the same time.

As she thought over her options, two things kept looking her in the face. Mac and Dillon Ryder. Finally, she was where she wanted to be in life. Surrounded by two men that seemed to care about her a great deal, but how was she going to be able to tell them her secret. Especially since Mac had just spent the last five minutes talking about the number one rule in a D/s relationship of being honest.

Feeling her emotions well up inside her, it was now or never. She needed to remind both of them of her plans. Whether she liked it or not she needed to tell them. Once that nasty situation was handled she would she how the guys took her news.

Maybe, just maybe they wouldn't want to start anything with her because she didn't know how her future was going to play out. She could still keep her secret hidden for now.

"Guys, I really love the fact that you feel the need to have a relationship with me, but I'm just not sure if I'm really ready for such a big endeavor."

Charlie watched as Dillon slowly let go of her legs, and slid off the sofa. Just feeling loss of his touch made her insides grow cold.

She could see it in his face; she had stung him deep down. He went from Mr. Happy to Mr. I'm going to rip your head off guy. Knowing that she needed to take control of the situation, Charlie put on her courtroom face.

Ms. Prosecutor.

She had showed them earlier this face and it worked for her then. She just hoped it worked now.

"Honesty is your number one rule right?"

"It is kitten. What do you need to tell us? I can see something is eating at you. I can tell by the way your holding your hands, if that were my head I'm sure you would have crushed by now." She was engaged in contemplation. She had to answer his question.

Charlie slowly took a deep breath in, stroke the side of her head, and without any more stalling, she said, "I'm not sure I'm staying in Crave."

She watched as Mac took a deep breath in, and Dillon paced around the living room. "I've already taken three months' bereavement time off from the law firm, my boss has been more than understanding, but I can tell his patience is running thin. I called the relator a month ago about putting the diner on the market. She thinks it will sell fast, but something deep down in my heart tells me that I should keep it and let someone manage it."

Neither guy said a word, they just stared at her, which kicked up Charlie emotions. She could already feel the tears beginning to form. *They just need to say it's okay to walk away. I'd be perfectly fine. Just walk away you two. I don't need you guys in my life, or do I?*

"I still don't know why my parents had to go and change their will. Everything was already set for Aunt Trudy to take over the diner. I can't tell you how surprised I was when Craig read my parents will stating that I was the sole beneficiary of everything."

"Why were you surprised, sweetheart? Your parents loved you dearly. For the past few years, your mother talked about if you could just come home. She missed you so much, she loved it when you Skype, but everyone could tell she needed to hold you, hug you, she couldn't do that via Skype. She praised you more than you'll ever know, but deep down she was missing her little girl."

"Oh god I never knew she was missing me that much." "Charlie, it wasn't just your mom, it was everyone town. When one of us leaves, it's a big deal. Look around how many people do you know of that have actually left town."

Charlie shrugged her shoulders as if she didn't really know.

"Let me tell you hum it's only been a handful. When someone leaves our community, it makes a large impact on everyone. Having you leave has touched everyone lives, having you back has brought happiness back into a sad situation. The first few weeks after your parent's death, it felt like the diner had died too.

Poor Gloria was lost, but you've given her direction again, and Greg well let's just say he's tried to steer Gloria in the correct direction. I don't know if either one of them know that they each have feelings for each other."

"Isn't it funny how others can see their attraction but neither one of them can. Just like us huh...it just taken us eight years to realize that you mean something to us, Charlie. I'm not willing to watch you walk again without giving it our best shot."

"We let you do that once before."

"Not again."

As his words let his mouth, she felt Macs lips gently touch hers. Feeling like she had never before, her heart exploded inside her chest. Thinking became impossible, all she could do was feel. She had to let go and let them both in, and in doing so she could possible heal her broken heart.

Rapidly beating faster than she had ever felt her heart beat before, she wasn't sure if she was having another panic attack or was it normal to feel this revved up.

Instead of pulling away, Charlie wrapped her arms around Mac neck. She was holding on for dear life. In an instant, she felt hands on her back and around her waist.

Dillon had re-joined them. She felt him nuzzle the side of her neck. She let a moan slip out of her mouth as Mac devoured her.

Never had she felt this relaxed or loved before. Feeling lost in the touches of these two men, she felt her pressures ease from her mind.

Riding the wave that was currently taking her farther and farther out to sea. She no longer felt as if she were drowning instead she was drifting peacefully along the calm deep blue sea.

Her two men were lifesavers.

When Mac broke off from her lips, she suddenly felt the loss of his touch. Never before had she wanted something so bad in her life, she now knew that she had to tell both of them about her secret, but her insides were telling her to go with moment. She wanted this feeling to last forever.

In order to survive this whirlwind she had to give it a chance to work. The back of her head she knew she still had just under a month before she had to make a decision about leaving Crave or going back to New York. *Why not see if something could work out between Mac and Dillon.*

Pulling away from his lips was a hard thing to do, but needing air to breathe was another thing. Both guys astounded her. They replaced it with a warm feeling.

Before we go any further, once you agree you'll be our submissive, that's if you agree. Dillon and I will guide you in every way possible." Charlie was already feeling like she was soaring, as if she had just drunk a whole bottle of wine.

What did she have to lose at this point? The worst would be calling everything to a halt after a months' time and heading back to New York.

"We need to hear you say yes before we go further. What that means Charlie, you will submit to us and only us. You'll let us take care of you and everything that you care about. Let us be in charge, you can sit back, and enjoy the ride, let your mind free it's self of all of your worries. The only thing that Mac and I ask that you be honest with us and to yourself. You need to trust that we have your best interest at heart." Dillon said.

Charlie starred at them, this had been her dream for so many years, to have someone take the responsibilities from her, and that's exactly what they were doing.

Both of them were willing to do just that. Her heart and soul rang out as she realized that her deepest dream had come true, Dillon and Mac wrapped their arms around her.

"We need to hear that you want this, Charlotte. You need to use your voice and say yes. You hold the key to your own happiness."

Before Dillon could get another word out of his mouth, she grabbed for both of their hands, knowing this was the start of her future. "I have a secret that I've been carrying around for so many years. I hope this doesn't change your minds about me. You said that I need to be honest, if this relationship is going to work.

"Correct."

"What ever happened in your past is in the past, Charlie, that doesn't change how Dillon and I feel about you. We've had these feeling since high school; nothing or anybody will ever change that."

"Whatever it is will work it out. Okay?"

Sighing, Charlotte took a deep breath in, watching her world around her, hoping that it didn't just implode.

"Back in high school do you remember a guy Carl Hughes?"

"Yeah he was on the football team with us. Isn't he the guy who left after graduation? Got in trouble and did some jail time in Baltimore for robbery."

"That's him." *Mr. Citizen of the year.*

"After, the big win over Hamilton High, everyone came back to the diner for pie and ice cream to celebrate the win. My mom always treated the team, she just loved that football was so important to everyone in town, so it became a thing for everyone to hang out after the games.

I guess it was around ten thirty when everyone started going home. I told my mom I would clean up, and close the diner myself. No big deal. I had done it hundreds of times.

Well after doing just that, I took out the trash and Carl was waiting for me by the dumpsters." Hesitating for just a second, tears began to stream down Charlotte's cheeks.

"That motherfucker didn't touch you, did he?" Mac yelled. "He threw me on the ground and rapped me.

Tears streamed down her face. Trying not to face either one of them, she closed her eyes.

Dillon jumped up from behind her; she could see the steam coming from his body. He was ready to rip apart anything that he could get his hands on.

The room started to spin; Charlotte could no longer focus on what was happening around her. All she could think about was the reaction that both men were having after telling them her secret. She had expected this reaction.

Slowly she slid off Mac's lap, before she could settle her wobbly legs on the floor; Dillon was at her side in an instant. He grabbed her and held on tight, the next thing she knew was Mac was at her back holding her too.

Both were saying things but all she could comprehend was, if the son of a bitch ever showed back up in Crave they would kill him. Suddenly her mind was no longer filled with hatred instead she felt the warmth again from her two men.

"Baby, don't cry we've got you. No one will ever hurt you again. As long as I live, I promise to protect you." Dillon whispered into her ear.

She'd had cried herself to sleep every night for the past eight years, she felt tonight would be no different. Or would it? Had she just heard Dillon correctly? Was he willing to accept her secret? He surely sounded pissed but it wasn't directed towards her.

Instead, his actions showed a concerned, caring, comforting man that would give his life to change what had happened to her. For years, she had been dealing with shock, denial, disbelief of what had really happened to her.

What she needed to focus on now was what Lisa, her therapist, had said to her. She needed to come to terms with what happened. She had done nothing to persuade her captive to force himself on her. She needed to move on with her life and in doing that she had to have a support team in place that she could go to when her self-esteem was low. She struggled with having people in her life that could help; she was going to turn that around starting now.

Letting these two fine, strong, handsome men in her inner circle was a huge first step. Tomorrow she would reconnect with a few girlfriends that she had shut out of her life, and make up for that girl time she so missed.

Feeling so empowered to do the things she had so wanted to do for the past few years squeezed at her chest. She had always known that she wanted to be loved by two men, and live the way her mother had lived, the sad factor that stung was that her parents wouldn't be by her side to see that dream come true, but somehow she knew that her mother had a hand in having her return to Crave County.

No longer would she be paralyzed by what had happened to her so many years ago. Just by telling Mac and Dillon, a weight had been lifted off her shoulders. Charlie no longer felt numb, like she had for so many years. The pain and memory would always be etched in her mind, but she didn't need to be haunted.

No more dwelling on the past she had to look for the future and they were both holding her securely in their arms. She would be there to love if they would have her. She had one more secret to share with them; she hoped that what she had to say wouldn't be a deal breaker.

"Guys, I feel like both of you have just opened up my eyes, it feels like I was blind to living, you have both made me realize that life is worth living for. I can finally see, I feel free, I know that most rape victims bounce back a whole lot faster than what I have, instead of healing I submerged myself in work. I need to put effort into healing, forgiving, and moving on. I've been officially given a second chance. I need to trust again. I'm going to need help on my bad days, therapist Lisa believes that I have two of the best support systems looking at the two of them. I just never thought I could ask for help." *I can't back down now. I can't lose them. Please don't leave me because I told them.*

She felt both of them tighten their grip on her. She never thought that she could felt as loved as she did this very moment. There was no possible way of stopping this feeling, she couldn't stop now, and she had to have both of them.

Time stood still as her two men held her tight. Love had waited its time; she was now ready to make her next move. Just as she was ready to tell both Mac and Dillon about her lack of sexual experience, she heard the front door swing open.

Startled by the sight of her Aunt Trudy, Doc Owens and June standing in her living room, Charlie struggled to break the hold that both of the Ryder brothers held around her. Just like a sneaky snake, instead she did it with grace, poise, and without any hissing.

Interrupted by visitors wasn't what Charlotte was looking forward to but she had to see what her family wanted them she would see to her own needs.

CHAPTER 9

Listening to June and Aunt Trudy go on and on about Charlotte's health became a little nauseating, all she could think about was her two men who at on each side of her stroking up and down her arms.

At first she felt a little weird sitting in front of her Aunt with her potential new family but hearing her and June laugh about how they have to pack up everything in her aunt's tiny red convertible had her mind refocused on tomorrow's picnic.

New life had surged through her since she had opened up to her men about being raped. She needed to do the same with her aunt and her future aunt. She would need all the support in the world if her plans were about to change.

Trying to think up a clever way to get just the women out of the living room, Charlotte walked towards both women and grabbed their hands, "I need help in the kitchen with something, and I could use your advice."

Right on cue, all three women went to the kitchen leaving their men sitting on the sofas.

Once in the room Charlotte went directly to the coffeemaker and turned in on. Thinking she could use a stiff cup of Joe to get her nerve up. In addition, if she had her way it would give her a little more energy for after her family left to be with her men.

"I called you both in her because I need to tell you both something that's been eating me alive. Turning towards her Aunt Trudy she said, "You know that I love you dearly, everything you have done for me growing up has meant the world to me. Even though you're not my mother I've always felt that you're my second mom."

"That's so wonderful to her Char. You've made me so proud that you considered me your second mom."

"You protected me when I needed you the most. Keeping my secret locked away in your heart, not telling a single soul, not even my mother hits me here." Charlotte pointed to her heart. "I know it must have been terribly hard for you, but I love you even more for protecting me."

"You're the daughter I couldn't have. You mean the world to me Charlotte. I'm just so glad that bastard is rotting away in a jail cell in Baltimore."

"What are the two of you talking about?" June piped up.

"What she's talking about, June, is I was raped by a guy in high school named Carl Hughes, just before my eighteenth birthday.

I asked my aunt to keep my secret from everyone. Thankfully, she was able to get me help when I most needed it, what I learned today was that she had to keep that locked away from her best friend, my mom.

I didn't know that in doing so that it caused a separation between the two of them. For that, I'm greatly sorry.

My insecurities took me away from my family, my home, and even from who I truly am. I thought I was damaged goods, but I now know that isn't the case. Instead, my virginity was taken from me. Not my life. I lost something greater though than my virginity and that was being able to spend time with my family. That thought will never leave my heart."

Both women rushed to Charlie's side as the tears slid down her face. She missed being held, the warmth that came off their bodies had been missed for far too long. Charlie made a silent note that she would cherish the time that she had with her family. She would make every minute count; she would no longer take things for granite anymore.

Drying her tears on the hem of her blouse, Charlie pulled away from both girls offering them the cup of coffee that she had first come in to the kitchen for.

Bringing up the picnic for tomorrow had the three women joking and laughing in no time at all. This was how things were supposed to be, happy, joyous, and fun, not the dreary shit that Charlie had drummed up in her head. That was going to change starting tonight. She'd had so many pent up emotions for so long she wasn't sure how she's react tomorrow with everyone around her.

She wasn't going to worry about that now, instead she was going to live in the moment and not look back over her shoulder anymore. Not everything in this world was a hundred percent perfect. She finally realized that now.

People could criticize, mock her, and even look at her funny, but that wasn't going to stop her from securing a future with Mac and Dillon. Not one inch of this earth was a perfect place or even had perfect people, for all that it is worth I'm not ashamed to say anymore that I'm not perfect.

Perfect is only in fairytales and the last time she looked she wasn't living in fairyland. No, she lived in the real world, where we have real problems, real issues. Dwelling on her rape would no longer cause her to get upset with herself.

"Instead I'm going to take my energy and start a law practice here in Crave and at the same time I'm going to make Maxwell's Diner the best fucking diner in the word. I can do this by making my parents proud. Even, though they are no longer here to see it. I know they'll be staring down from heaven to guide me when I fall."

After spending what felt like hours going over how tomorrow would worked out with all of her staff and family, Charlie watched her aunt leave with her new family.

Boy she did look extremely happy being with Jane and Doc, if anyone could bounce back from being abused she knew that Trudy was a fighter. She'd take on the meanest bull in a rink faster than you could blink your eyes, or gut a man without getting blood on her hands; she was her fierce aunt, and protector.

Seeing her aunt this happy gave her the courage to move forward. And that's exactly what she planned to do, but first she needed a hot bath to soothe her built up sexual frustrations. She was so thankful when Dillon made his way to the bathroom to start her bath water. She could get used to be pampered.

CHAPTER 10

After soaking for what seemed like days, Charlie ventured back to the living room where both of her men were watching TV. Feeling a little apprehensive if she should make the first move or should she just see how the rest of the night would play out for them, slowly she walked over to the rocking chair and plopped down making a girlish giggle.

I may not know everything about being with a guy, hell even a Dom. But looking at these two delicious looking guys has me all hot and bothered. This has to be a good sign.

Charlie looked around the large room; she could see her mother in every detail. Thankfully, her mother had a distinguished eye for fashion. Every knickknack had its place. Pictures lined the wood mantel above the fireplace. The walls were a light shade of heather green with the crown molding painted in a white. *What would this room look like if I changed up the colors to something more my style? Even though I know my mom had great style, I need to make it my own.* That is exactly what she planned on doing, making this house her home.

Seeing that Charlie had taken a long time in the bath gave Mac and Dillon sometime to figure out their next plan of action. Knowing now that Charlie had been raped, by one of their fucking friends, had filled their souls with an anger that neither one of knew they had.

A demon had been locked away in both of their souls, revenge had never been either of their demeanors, but seeing how dickhead Carl had caused pain to Charlie would have them on high alert for the near future.

For that reason, they needed to redirect their original plan. They couldn't just push themselves onto her. Slow had a better ring than fast and hard.

Most likely Charlie hadn't had any type of sexual experience with a man since her rape, left both guys thinking how they could satisfy their sexy kitten.

First, they needed to pay close attention to how she showed her emotions, once she came back into the room. If she expressed happiness, they would proceed to the next level in their relationship.

She would be a force to be reckoned with and both guys were definitely up for the challenge. Watching her perch herself in the chair and not on the sofa between the two of them gave Mac the perfect idea. They would need to take care of her needs first and later she could take care of theirs.

Charlie had waited so long for this moment to happen. Seeing both of her men looking at her with their primal stares should have scared her, instead, it did the opposite; it turned her desires on even more. Something that had been turned off for so long. Charlotte placed her hands on her quivering stomach. She felt like butterflies swam around in her belly, giving her a sense of insecurity.

She smoothed her damp palms down over her robe, forcing her to get a grip of what was about to happen. The only noise heard was her father's antique grandfather clock that she had sent from Germany on their last birthday. She heard TIC, TOCK of the clock, making her heart beat at the same rate.

She was about to enter into the forbidden world of an amazing, alternative lifestyle.

Would being loved by these two men bring light to the darkness that had shadowed over her for so long? Her life had been a living hell for all these years, she was about to find out how happy life could be.

She was stepping out of her comfort zone, letting the two men be her guiding hands. Charlotte exhaled deeply and steadied her nerves. She still heard the loud sound of the clock. TICK, TOCK.

She had wanted this for so long. Now that she was about to have both of them, fear consumed her brain. How was this really going to work? Before she let her fear get the best of her, she felt it was best to let them know what she was feeling.

They had both told her that they were going to take things slow and she surely hoped that meant with sex too. Not being with a man in a long time, she was sure her vagina needed to be worked or played with before she could let herself fly.

She heard Mac begin to growl from across the room. She took that as his way of saying that she was getting ready to be plowed down by the king of jungle. She heard a similar noise come from Dillon this must be their way in saying she is about to be devoured by them. Excitement rose higher in her veins, no longer would she worry about what was going to happen she would just let them take her to a happy place that she had been longing for.

The robe that was wrapped around her body as her security blanket was suddenly being taken off her shoulders. All of her will power was being stripped from her.

"Baby, are you with us?" Not wanting to be lost totally she shook her head in a gesture that said yes.

"No baby before we go any further, we need to hear you say that this is what you want from us. Do you remember the phrase about safe-words and when you should use them?" Timidly she shook her head again.

"Green means, GO, and GO, And GO. Yellow means, slow down, we need a break. Red means, STOP." The inflection in her voice told both of then she was more than ready.

"Our girl is a fast learner. What color are you now kitten?"

She had heard him call her kitten earlier at the hospital, she was surprised when it turned her on even more, and she could feel the wetness on her cloth panties. She felt her face heat up as the word "Green" slipped from her mouth. They must have heard it her voice because both of them chuckle at the same time.

Never had her heart pounded so erratically before, but at the softness of their tone, slowly she closed her eyes and she just felt. *I surrender my mind, body, and soul to both of them.*

She felt Dillon's hands caress her neck, as Mac captured her mouth. Slowly feeling both of them at the same time send sparks of fireworks in her head. She could hear them going on and on about how beautiful she was, how pleased they are at how well she was doing. All Charlie could do was moan out her happiness with each, touch, caress, and kiss they both gave her.

Both of them were making it so damn hard for her to think, all she could do was... Just feel as she let a squeal out of her mouth. Before she knew sit it her nightgown had been removed and was sitting in the rocking chair now with just her panties and bra on.

What was so amazing she didn't mind being almost naked in front of these two. It's like her body had been washed away with being damaged goods and now it's back to being pure again. A clean feeling, not the sterile kind, but more like when you wash the sheets on your bed and you climb in the first time.

Beads of sweat form along the top of her forehead as each guy slowly works their way down to her breasts. If this is what her mother talked about being sandwiched between two hunky guys swirled through her mind. *I would've done it a long time ago*.

Bliss was starting to set in, no more fears, no more worries, just the constant stimulation that each man gave her. *What a fucking delicious feeling. Please don't stop, I can't get enough.*

"Dillon, bro can you smell our girl?"

"She smells like the most delicious peach, man. Her pussy is glistening with her cream waiting for our tongues to lick her dry." Hearing her groan told both of them that she was needy. They watched as she closed her eyes, they could tell she was riding a wave taking her higher and higher. Charlotte's face bore what was the most precious expression either one of them had ever seen. She was crossing over to a stage of bliss, "No time like the present to introduce her to having her sweet, wet pussy eaten." Mac whispered.

"I think our girl is going to love being our desert for tonight."

Ah, I think you're right. Did you just hear her purr her response to your question?"

Slowly Mac placed his hand on both of her knees, working his way up her thighs massaging her now relaxed inner muscles. Both men assaulted her sexual desires at the same time.

"Kitten are you still with Dillon and me?

"I'm green, Sir."

"Good girl. I'm very impressed you remember to add the sir at the end of your answer. For that my little kitten, how's about I give you a reward."

"I think I love the sound of that, Sir, my insides are burning up with so much pent up desire. I can honestly say I've never felt this good before, Sir."

"That's music to my ears, sweetie." Dillon Crooned.

She purred a little louder when Dillon slowly took hold of her chin and tilted it back to rest on the headrest of the rocking chair. He watched as her eyes dilated. Kissing the side of her throat, Dillon liked to mark his woman when he played with them. He hadn't expressed that to Charlie yet, so instead he stroked her neck with his long tongue. He would mark her though with a passionate love mark.

At the same time, he knew that his brother was getting closer and closer to her pussy. She tried to arch her pussy closer to Mac's mouth. Dillon said to her to "lay still kitten all good things come to those that wait for what they are given."

Signing slightly both guys just chuckled as Charlie slid back in place on the rocking chair.

"That's a good girl. Can you feel Mac's mouth getting closer to your hot, wet pussy, sweetheart?"

"I feel his hot breath getting closer and closer. I'm not sure how much more I can take, Sir. He's driving me totally insane. Please, just take me Sir."

Just as the words left Charlie's mouth, Mac parted her swollen lips his both of his hands, he blew a stream of air on her pink, plump, swollen pussy. He watched as her labia quivered, and her clit stretched. He could tell that she was getting close to having her first orgasm in a long time.

Hopefully he could have her coming all over his cock in the future, either while she sucked his brother's cock or was fucked up the ass. He felt Charlie's body begin to twitch; this was the true sign that she was close.

Dillon was licking and sucking on her neck at the same time that Mac was sucking on her clit. Dillon could tell that she was getting close. He whispered in her ear, "Kitten, come for us baby." Without hesitation, they felt their girl let loose. She screamed loud enough to wake up the dead.

"Let it go baby we've got you." Her juices coated Mac's tongue and lips as he sucked in as much of her cream as possible.

"That's it kitten, give us your pleasure." Dillon said to her in a soft growl.

"Oh god, I'm coming, Sirs. Please don't stop. I need more. Please, I need more."

Swirling his tongue in and around her clit, Mac had Charlie going off within seconds. It had been a long time since a woman had given them this gift. They were truly blessed with her act of submission.

CHAPTER 11

Feeling large hands pick her up out of the rocking chair, she wasn't sure where they were taking her, but she hoped that was to her bed. She was sure that this was the happiest she had been in years. No longer did she feel like a weight was wrapped around her heart. Instead, she felt alive and free of her past.

"Sweetheart which room is yours?"

"Last door on the left." Dillon gingerly laid her down on the center of her bed. She heard water running, trying not to open up her eyes, she felt Mac spread her legs. He ran a warm facecloth over her swollen pussy. Slowly he cleaned her just as if she was a baby, while Dillon held her tightly.

Once her sex was cleaned and dry, Mac returned to her other side; she felt the bed dip as he slid under the covers and held her tight. Dillon held her from her back, until the three of them drifted off to sleep.

As the light from the morning sun shinned in from her bedroom window, Charlie slowly opened her eyes to find two gorgeous hunks, sleeping in her bed. *They stayed. I can't believe they stayed.*

Pinching her thigh just to make sure that she was dreaming, pain seared under the skin where she had just inflicted pain. *Nope this is real. The Ryder twins in my fucking bed.* Doing a happy dance was all Charlie could think about doing. But no, she didn't want to wake up her two men. Instead, she just lay in bed staring at their hot sexy bodies.

Neither one had taken off his clothes. Somehow, Charlie now had her nightgown back on. She remembered being carried to bed last night, naked. They must have dressed her after she fell asleep.

She sat up, still a little fuzzy headed but not in a bad way. Slipping from the grips of her two sleeping men. She quickly made her way to the bathroom. She was surprised that she had her nightgown; her guys must have felt it was important enough for her to have it on. That thoughtful gesture deeply touched her heart.

Looking in the large mirror, she no longer saw the withdrawn, insecure, depressed woman. She had the look of a confident, bright eyed, spunky fiery red head that she used to be. She was a woman with a purpose in life.

Giggling like a schoolgirl in love, she pulled her robe off the hook and went down stairs to the kitchen. Starting a new day, a new chapter in her life gave Charlie the push to make the call to her employer. Even though it was a holiday, her boss still picked up his calls. After a few minutes discussing the situation with him, she gave her resignation. She would also be sending an official email on Monday with her immediate resignation. *Damn he took that well.*

The sun was shining bright, the birds were chirping, the only thing missing now was her morning tea. Somehow, she had a feeling that Mac, and Dillon would require something more substantial than tea.

She knew they both were coffee drinkers, black and two sugars. Thank goodness she had all the condiments for a good hot cup of Joe. She made a mental note; *find out what brand they liked she would need to stock up on some of their favorite things.* Especially since her pantry was so bare, having all of the mother's favorite recipes she would start cooking on a regular basis.

No more starving herself when she felt depressed, her body couldn't handle it. She learned that her support group would be helpful, to pull her through her deep dark dreary days. She was sure she would have them in the future, now she knew how to process things a little differently that's all.

She pulled three mugs from a shelf, filled two with coffee, and hers with tea. She had popped a few pieces of toast in the toaster and pulled out a jar of her mother's homemade strawberry jam.

It was times like these when she saw something that had touched her parents so deeply that it would remind her that they were no longer present with her anymore. Instead, she had to live with happy memories of her past. Tears filled her eyes when she thought about how she much she truly missed her mother. Her mother would not be present for the happy days to come, her wedding, the birth of grandchildren; they would always be deep in her heart.

Instead of dwelling on how life used to be, she would make new happy memories by keeping a journal that she could share with them when she visited their graves.

Shaking her head brought her back to the present. Today is going to be the start of something good, danced in her head, she remember her mother often saying, "Life is too short to worry about stupid things. Have fun. Fall in love, regret nothing and don't let people bring you down."

With that thought lodged in Charlie's head, she picked up the tray and proceeded upstairs to her sleeping hunks. When she entered the room, Mac was just waking up. She went to set down the tray on her nightstand. Dillon had told her that he wasn't a morning person and liked to sleep in late. Mac on the other hand was an early riser. The sheer contrast between both of them was night and day when it came to their sleeping habits. Just from being with them one night, she could already tell that Mac was a cuddlier and Dillon liked to be cuddled.

Three of them sharing her queen size bed, didn't give them much room for spreading out. They would need to have something a little larger. Her parents bed was a California King and fit her parents well, another shopping list item for the future.

"Good morning beautiful," came from Mac's mouth as he sat up stretching and yawning.

She heard moaning coming from Dillon's side of the bed. "You know some of us are not god damn morning people"

"Look sleeping beauty woke-up on the wrong side of the bed." Mac shouted out.

"You don't need any more sleep, it's a beautiful day. Can't you hear the birds chirping?"

"No kitten, all I can hear is the inside of my eye lids saying they need about another three hours of rest."

Both Mac and her chuckled as they listened to Dillon give them all the reasons in the world why it was way too early for them to be having this discussion.

"I can't wait to get to the 4th of July picnic. I'm so excited my insides feel like they're going to burst for joy. I haven't felt like this in years. I'm just so happy I have the two of you to celebrate it with."

"Baby what time is it?" Dillon growled.

"Six am."

"You woke me up at the crack ass of dawn to get ready for the picnic. Are you crazy woman? Let me get this straight. The picnic doesn't start for another six hours." She watched as Dillon slowly picked up her pillow and threw it at her. Protecting her face with her hand, she snatched the pillow midair, without even a second guess, she jumped up on the bed between her two men and swatted Dillon on the top of his head with the pillow.

Knowing that both guys liked to play games, they surely were in a playful mood this morning. The next thing she heard was "pillow fight" both guys attacked her, "game on" came squeaking from her tiny mouth.

They picked her up and threw her down on the bed, while each guy took turns tickling, giving her Indian rug burns up and down her arms, blowing bubbles on her belly, and kissing her wildly with shear hot passion. The laughter of three happy people echoed throughout the room.

"Look Mac, I think Dillon needs to roll back over and go back to sleep for a little while longer, you and I can share some toast in bed. Maybe just maybe I might drop a few crumbs on his side and he'll roll around, smashing them on his back."

"Oh, no you don't, kitten, you woke me up now you need to feed me. Baby.

"Is that so?"

"You woke the beast inside of me up, seeing your shinning face has me think of all different ways I want your pretty mouth, being used this morning. You got all the pleasure last night. This morning I think it should be all about your Masters pleasure. What do you think Mac, having our bubbly, happy little sub wrap her succulent lips around our cocks? Doesn't it send shivers down your balls?"

"You do have a point there brother. Seeing our submissive as cheerful as she is this morning, we could have her use some of that energy she's been storing up on both of us."

She'd never been submissive to a man before last night, so why did the thought of being at Dillon's and Mac's complete and total mercy cause her entire body to clench with need. Deep down she already knew that answer, she just needed to hear from their mouths say she was needed for them and them only.

Dillon yawned as he rolled off the bed, dropping his jeans to the floor. Surprised that he wasn't wearing any underwear. Going commando was definitely his style. She wondered if Mac did the same.

Charlie's eyes were glued to one spot and one spot only. His nether region. Dillon did a great job at manscaping. Not a single hair was noted around his penis or balls. What caught her eye was a shiny silver ball that pierced the head of his penis.

Making a loud slurping noise, loud enough that both guys could hear. Charlie watched as Mac undressed as well. Seeing the deep purple swollen head of his penis with the identical piercing made her mouth water even more. *Fucking delicious...*

After seeing several piercings during her visit to a dungeon back in New York, Charlie searched on line and saw different types of body piercing. She wondered what it would feel like having a Jacob's ladder piercing rub her insides. Everything that she read about them said they brought more sexual stimulation than an un-pierced penis. She wouldn't have to wait much longer to experience just that. She had that funny feeling stir to life again in her pussy. *I love the way these two make my insides come to life.*

"Look baby, you woke me up," Mac said with a funny tone to his voice. Before she could answer him, Dillon said he needed a little more time to wake up his dragon since he was not a morning guy.

Mac took her hands in his and repositioned her on the floor. Guiding her slowly to her knees, she submitted to a position she had never been in before. Both guys stood directly in front of her stroking up and down their long shafts. With each stroke, she could see their manly shafts getting harder and harder with each fierce stroke.

"Are you okay, Kitten?"

She loved it when they called her kitten, sweetheart, or baby. It made all of her fears disappear. She finally felt alive. Only the three of them existed when they used that term with her. Nothing else matter, the world could be exploding around them and all she would care about is how they addressed her needs.

"Yes, Sirs. I'm good. Green as summer grass."

"Our girl deserves a reward for answering in the correct manner."

She felt blessed at that moment hearing how pleased there were with her answer sent goose bumps up and down her spine. Mac reached down as stroked the top of her head as Dillon placed his lips on hers. She moaned as he took her mouth. Surrendering to his touch put her in a very happy place. She had longed for this place. And now that she had finally found this place, she didn't want to leave.

Feeling Dillon remove his lips from hers, instantly she felt the loss of being connected to him. As soon as he was gone, Mac took his place. It only took a few seconds before she slipped back into that happy place. She as if she were floating in the clouds, soaring high above the clouds just as a beautiful condor would. Circling around, she found just what she was looking for, and that had been starring her in the face. Her two men.

The grace and beauty that a condor used when soaring above high in the sky was the same grace a poise she was using this very moment to capture what she wanted out of life.

Happiness, love, and sense of belonging were the three things she had searched for all of her life. She had finally found the two people that gave that to her. Her body felt weightless as she continued to soar higher and higher.

Mac released her lips in the same manner as Dillon had. She needed to stay connected with the two of them. She looked at both of them with the most beautiful smile. Her lips were wet from their passionate kisses.

She drew her tongue up to her lips wetting them with more of her saliva. She needed no further encouragement. She reached for Mac's cock with her right hand. Never had she done something so primal before. She gave him a slight squeeze around his girth. Releasing just a drop of clear liquid.

Hearing his breathing speed up told her that she was doing the correct thing. She placed her hot mouth over Mac's cock, giving it a kiss. She had read that men loved to be licked, teased, and stroked on just the tip, so without any hesitation she replayed over and over in her head, lick, tease, and stroke.

Hearing Dillon give her words of encouragement sent her into orbit. She swirled her tongue up and down his shaft wetting him with her salvia.

Pre-cum leaked from the tip giving her a special treat that she quickly licked, like a lollipop. She had never tasted anything so wonderful in her life. All that played in her head was the commercial with the owl, *how many licks does it take to get to the center of the lollipop.*

Forcefully, she licked and licked trying to get to the center of the tootsie pop. She wasn't satisfied with just one lick, same as the owl. She was being a greedy girl, and wanted it all. She had to get to the center of Mac's core. She needed to satisfy him as they did to her last night.

Mac groan filled the room in pure satisfaction as she sucked his cock deeper into her mouth.

"That's it baby take me deeper into your hot mouth." Scooting just a little closer, Dillon spread his legs wider. Mac commanded her to play with Dillon's balls as she sucked his cock deeper and deeper down to the root of his shaft. She must have liked what she was doing because she started to purr, just as she did last night as they pleasured her pussy.

She was experiencing the most erotic delight of her life, pleasuring two guys at once. She never thought she would be so in-tuned to two guys at the same time. All of her fears had vanished, she no longer had issues with trust, and her job was to please. She surrendered her will over to both of them. Her mind, body, and soul were theirs.

Working her mouth on Mac's penis and her hands on Dillon's penis didn't take her long at all, getting her guys fully erect and ready to blow their loads.

"Baby, I'm not going to last much longer. I'm going to come down your throat. I want you to drink every last drop. Once I'm done, I want you to do the same to Dillon. Do you understand kitten?"

"Oh, yes, Sir." She moaned in pleasure.

She felt her warm juices coming from her pussy sliding down to her panties. Wetting them just as she was last night. She was filled with lust, desire and love, never had she felt this way before. All she knew that she never wanted this feeling to end.

Wanting to please them, she went deeper and deeper down on Mac's cock until it felt like she was going to gag. She heard Dillon say, "Baby. Breathe through your nose. You're fine. So good." She was sure that Mac's cock was tapping her tonsils.

She listened to both of their words of encouragement and focused on pleasuring Mac's cock. She heard Mac moan, as he did, she felt warm come fill her mouth, spurts of come emptied from his cock into the back of throat.

"That's it, baby, drink all of me." Swallowing as fast as she could, trying not to lose any of his come. Charlie had never felt as alive as she did in that moment; the two of them had bonded in a way she had never thought could be possible. After a few minutes of holding Mac's penis in her mouth he started to soften, he told her to remove her mouth from his penis and take Dillon's cock in her mouth as she just did to him.

As she slid from one cock to another, she felt more moisture running down the inside of her legs. She tried to close her legs, so that neither of her men could see the wetness coming from her arousal. Before she could press her legs together, she felt Mac's hands pushing them back open.

Never had she felt so wet in her life, she wouldn't have a need for lube like most women needed to enjoy sex. She had a natural lubricant that had been stored up for so many years. And now that her body started producing it, she wasn't sure if it would stop.

She felt Dillon get harder as she did the same thing to his cock, lick, tease, and stroke. Before she knew it she felt Mac between her legs, he took his teeth and ripped her underwear off from around her mound. His tongue hit her sex, and she soared even higher.

Trying not to forget that she had Dillon's cock in her, she'd hate to accidentally bite down. Feeling Mac swirl his tongue on her clit was super erotic in her mind. She was most sure she had just died and gone to sexual heaven. Nothing had ever felt this good.

Just when she thought she couldn't take anything more she felt Dillon's come hit the back of her throat, as her body started to shake a quiver, she moaned around him as she came, and how she never wanted them to stop or leave her.

She was sure she was speaking in some form of tongues, or having and outer body experience. She let Dillon's cock fall from her mouth, when she felt two sets of hands picking her up and placing her back on the bed.

Her eyes shut as her head hit her pillow. What felt like forever being asleep was only about an hour? She was surprised to find that both guys where laying on one on each side of her, holding her tight.

ABIGAIL LEE JUSTICE

Mac and Dillon watched as their beautiful girl fell asleep in both of their arms. She had surrender to their will, by letting all of her fears, worries, and pain was away from her mind. She had trusted them with a gift that she had never given to anyone else and that was her mind, body, and soul. They had finally found their missing puzzle piece. Neither one had ever experience the kind of connection with another person as they did with Charlie.

Dillon now had no reason to leave Crave County and every reason to stay. Her name was Charlotte Maxwell; hopefully someday soon it would be Mrs. Charlotte Maxwell Ryder if he had his way. He would take her down to the courthouse and do the right thing by making her theirs.

He just had to make sure that Mac was on the same page.

"Are you thinking what I'm thinking, bro?"

"Yeah, she's the one."

"Ah, sure is."

"I can't wait to show her off today at the picnic."

"Me too, bro, me too."

"Yesterday while I was fishing, I thought it was time for me to move on without you. I was ready to pack up and leave Crave County. After I took one look at her, I couldn't make myself think that again. She's what we've been missing for all these years.

"I have a feeling we're what been missing from her life. I just hope she sees it too."

"I know she does, just by the way she looks at both of us. I bet once she sees everyone today it's going to seal the three of us together. She has a glow about her that she didn't have before. She's more beautiful than she was in high school I just wish we could have saved her from being raped by that douche-bag. If I ever see him, I swear he'll never be able to hurt another woman again."

"We have the same feelings then. Do you think our girl's going to like going to The Farm in the future? Or do you think will be able to spice it up in the bedroom only?"

"I have a feeling now that her sexual appetite has been woken up, when she talks to her girlfriends, I bet she'll be begging us take her there. All she has to do is talk to Gloria for more than two seconds and she'll have her dressed to kill by the time we can get our leathers on."

"That reminds me. Bryce and Lexi are coming into town for the picnic, fireworks, and then a demo at the club. I should text him and tell him that I booked his room at the club, and have everything he specifically asked for waiting in the room."

"Do you think our girl will mind if we take her back to our place, I'm not sure if my back can take this tiny ass bed with the three of us in?"

"God I hope so, my arms went numb last night trying not to move."

"Let's wake her up first, she's going to need to eat, we can run by our place get some fresh clothes. We can show her around, and then we can go and meet everyone at the picnic."

"Sounds like you have it all planned out. Leave it to my big brother to have a plan."

"Wait, I'm only two minutes older than you."

"Still that makes you my older, wiser brother."

"Just think when were old and grey, rocking on the front porch with our girl in between us you'll still be older than all of us."

"You know in a way that doesn't sound half bad. The three of us growing old together. Mom and dads are going to be so happy when we show her off today. I just wish her parents were here to see how happy she is."

"Yeah that sucks, but at least we have the memories of them.

CHAPTER 12

After waking up from her morning delight with her guys, they took her to their place. She was surprised how nice and clean everything was. Each room showed off a little flair for each one of them.

The kitchen shined with all of the stainless steel appliances. It was amazing that she saw her reflection for the first time in the glass of the microwave door. She saw a vibrant, women with the clearest green eyes, and a smile plastered across her face. Could she really be feeling this happy over two guys? She pinched herself again making sure this wasn't a big nasty dream. *Nope not a dream.*

The guys had showed her the master bedroom, which had never been used. They told her, after the house was built several years ago, they made a pack with each other that when the time was right, and when they found the woman for the both of them, only then would they use the master bedroom. They left her in the master bedroom as they both went and took a shower in their rooms that they were currently using.

Everything in the big room had been arranged for the three of them just perfectly. A floral sofa set off in the corner of the room. A large bay window with a sitting area looking out over thirty-five acres of land gave the perfect morning view when sipping a cup of coffee. She could picture herself sitting on the ledge watching the snow fall on a cold winter's morning cuddled up with one of her mother's quilts. Decorated lamps sat on top of the two nightstands at the head of the bed.

In the center of the room was a large four-poster bed, not sure of the size, but she could already tell it was much larger than a king size bed. Both of her guys were at least six feet five inches if not taller. They must have had the bed specially made with their heights in mind. The white comforter, with pink and blue throw pillows were scattered at the head of the bed, must have been picked out by a woman because this was the only area in the house that showed a women's touch.

Above the bed, hung a picture frame with the words written, "Happiness isn't about getting what you want all the time. It's about loving what you have and being grateful for it."

She had seen the same words written above her parent's bed. Tears streamed down her face when she finally realized how withdrawn from the world she had been. Memories flooded her mind of what she had done to so many people.

Her parents must have felt bad when their only daughter left them, she could still see their faces when they shut her car door and waved good-bye.

Knowing that she sacrificed her friendship with her aunt by having her keep her secret. Isolating herself from her true friends. Life wasn't really worth losing the people that truly love you if you aren't at least happy with in yourself first resonated in her soul. Never again would she take little things for granted. She was going to look the bull in the eyes and charge for what she wanted out of life.

She needed to build a foundation first and grow from that. Her solid rock foundation wasn't just one man, but it was two. Just like so many other families in Crave County, she would follow in the footprints of her parents and her great grandparents.

She'd bet that their mom had something to do with the decorations in this room. Everything in each of the rooms was placed strategically just like in her parents place. It had a definitive touch of a woman. A soft, passionate, kind touch.

The only thing that was missing was the last piece of the puzzle, and that was her. They had told her on the drive over that they had never brought a woman to their home before. She felt all tingly inside that she would be the first and only women to call this their home.

She walked into the spacious bathroom, no detail had been spared, a long counter with three sinks, three mirrors and largest walk in shower that looked just like the one in her parents bathroom. Off to the corner was a sunken in Jacuzzi tub big enough to fit at least eight people.

Everything was brightly decorated with a neutral wheat tone. A large sky window opened up the entire ceiling to let in the morning sun. Or when soaking in the tub you could gaze at the stars.

Walking back into the bedroom she looked around the room again, she finally saw the bigger picture; home is where the heart is, and happiness steams from the home. She dried her tears with the hem of her sundress and waited for her two men. Curled up on their bed.

All she could do is laugh, how stupid she had been for so long, she not only separated herself from her family, but she segregated herself from friends, and the people who loved her. Starting today, that would change. Hearing her guys come back in the room, she quickly sat up.

"What's our girl thinking? I can see the wheels just a turning and turning."

"I have been so blind, for so many years, I can't believe how I've isolated myself from the living world. I ran away to New York so I didn't have to face my worst demons, which wasn't Carl Hugh. You know for all these years I saw myself as damaged goods. I never saw the good in anything.

I'm a smart, educated woman, who let a douche-bag get away with raping me. I didn't even go to the police to press charges. Hell I didn't even tell my parents because I was so worried how people would look at me. I didn't see the good in letting people know what he had done to me. I saw only the bad.

Taking a deep breath in Charlie had to get this off her chest so that she could move on from this tragedy. "I just hope he didn't do this to anyone else."

"Baby you have our promise that no matter what happens to you in the future, you'll never need to worry about how we look at you. No one should ever feel damaged especially when something traumatic happens to them. We stand here next to you as your partners, friends, lovers, Masters and someday real soon as your husbands."

Hearing Mac say the kindest words had tears streaming down her face. She had always felt alone; no longer did she have that feeling. She was being surrounded by love.

Happiness came in all shapes, sizes and structure, looking up at these two hunks of men brought each of them into a complete circle.

The three of them joined hands at that very moment. They completed the circle, before they came along it was just her, and no one else, except for her hidden demons. Even her family hadn't completed that circle for her.

Thinking back to everything they had talked about yesterday about being submissive, she finally realized that she had been being submissive to her demons letting them run her life, and not the other way around. She'd never been submissive to a man before so when she thought about being submissive to Mac and Dillon her entire body clenched with a need to be filled.

CHAPTER 13

She had never poured out her soul as she had for the last few minutes. She needed something else to tie her to them more permanently. She realized that they hadn't made love to her, yet. They had pleasured her, which was spectacular. But she still needed something else to bond them together forever.

Taking a deep breath in, she peeled off her sundress, removed her panties and bra and sank down to her knees as gracefully as the condor she already knew she was. She tilted her head slightly from her neck down, placing her chin on her chest. She waited for just a few seconds, then she said, "Make love to me. I need to have you both inside of me to feel whole again."

She heard them rustling with their clothes. She felt two sets of strong hands pick her up and place her on the center of the bed. Feeling the bed dip on both sides of her told her that both men were at her sides. Her heart was beating a mile a minute, she felt as if she were going to have a heart attack, but that was suddenly went away when she felt Mac's lips capture hers.

His kisses were the most passionate, warm expressions that a man had ever given to her. Her toes curled when his tongue danced in her mouth. She felt Dillon's strong hands on her right breast, he was massaging around her swollen nipples, with his strong calloused fingers. At the same time Mac's sucked his was down her neck.

She was lost to their feel and touch. Being in the here and now having her two condors take her for theirs was all she wanted. She felt Mac kneel between her legs, she dropped her knees open so that he had a direct opening to her sex. Dillon handed him a condom, she watched as Mac slowly sheathed himself. He reached between her sex with two fingers and gathered up some of her natural juices. He slowly took her juices and coated the outside of the condom.

She was lost to both of them. She was in her happy, floaty, place.

"Baby are you sure you want me inside of you?"

Without hesitation Charlie's answer was, "I've never wanted something so bad in my life. I want you both more than my next breath of air. I want this so bad, I finally see where my heart belongs and that is with both of you."

Tears stung the side of her face. Mac slowly placed the tip of his penis to her opening, while Dillon took her mouth at the same time.

She felt every inch of him pushing his way into her vagina. She had never felt something so wonderful before. There was no pain, no ripping or tearing like she experienced while being raped, instead she felt warmth. Mac rolled both of them onto their right side. Dillon whispered in her ear that he loved her, he told her he was going to place some numbing lube on her backside. She gave out a loud scream when she felt his finger breach her tight hole. He worked the lube in and out for a few minutes. All at the same time, Mac slowly moved in and out of her wet, slick, pussy. She was surprised how fast her ass got numb, she didn't even feel Dillon's fingers anymore.

"Kitten are you ready to take off into outer space?"

"Oh, god I feel so good. I can't even imagine what it is going to feel like when I have you both inside of me. Sirs make me yours."

"Kitten you were already ours," she felt the tip of his cock, slowly slide in her ass, while Mac slowly slid out of her pussy just to the tip, they played a game of in and out until she screamed that she could take it anymore, and that she was going to come.

Both guys told her to take them with her, they were all on the ride of their life. No longer would they be apart. They would always be joined by this moment in time. Feeling like she couldn't hold back any longer, Charlie soared above the clouds with her two condors above her, guiding the way. Her happiness was all that mattered; she now knew that they would provide, protect, and serve her for as long as they lived.

Each one of them made that promise to each other. She no longer felt like she was alone. She was alive, and survived a horrible thing. No longer would she surrender to her demons, instead she would surrender to her two masters, Mackenzie and Dillon Ryder.

Mac growled as his seed coated the inside of her pussy, and Dillon let his seed go inside of her ass. The three of them had sealed their circle once and for all.

The only thing left was to enjoy each other, making memories of their own.

Mac slowly withdrew his semi erect penis, she watched him walk over to the bathroom. When he reappeared, he held a warm wet washcloth in his hand. Dillon slowly pulled out of her backside. Mac took his hands and washed her completely. He looked at her pussy and ass closely making sure that they had causes her any damage to her swollen tissues.

Once she was all cleaned up, they lay across the bed and cuddled. They told her how much they loved her and how they couldn't wait to spend the rest of their lives together.

She had found bliss in the arms of her two lovers. She was happy, safe and secure for the first time in a long time.

"You know, I'd love to stay in bed for the rest of the day, but I'm afraid my presence would be missed today at the picnic."

"Look Dillon we turned our girl into a sex machine, she'd rather be in bed with us."

"Mackenzie Ryder, I didn't say such a thing. I said we need to get dressed so that I can show you two off at the picnic. I have half the mind to put a sign around both of your necks saying, hands off their mine."

Both guys busted out laughing at what had just slipped out of Charlie's mouth. She was back to her joking was just like she had been in high school. That was the girl they fell in love with so many years before.

"Is that so, baby, we thought we might have more time, but seems that you're putting signs around our necks, why don't we put something around yours."

"You already did last night when you put a hickey on my neck."

"Well I did do that. Didn't I?" Dillon pointed to her neck. "Wait until I permanently mark you as mine."

She picked up her underwear but before she could put them back on Mac grabbed them out of her hands and told her that she would no longer need this pair, they were his. At first, she protested when he told her that his submissive no longer required her pussy to be cover with cloth.

She didn't even question his statement, because she trusted that he had her best interests at heart. She liked hearing the words his submissive. Dillon handed her the sundress that was at the foot of the bed.

"Dresses from now on my dear, we don't like pants," she had noticed that most women especially her Aunt Trudy always wore dresses or skirts.

"Better access, baby, to what belongs to Dillon and me."

"Got it Sirs, I think I might need a shopping trip or two because I only have pant suits in my closets."

"Not to worry, shopping trip Monday morning. You plan it and we'll take care of the rest."

"You don't need to take care of me like that, Dillon. I'm a big girl."

"Kitten, we know you're a big girl but we like spoiling what is ours."

"I think I can get used to feeling this way," before she could get another word out of her mouth, she felt Mac snack her bottom. "OUCH, what was that for?"

"That, kitten was your first punishment for not trusting your Masters to take care of what is ours."

"She needs to talk to the girls today at the picnic to get a crash course in this whole D/s thing. That way she doesn't make that mistake again.

"Now baby, go thank Master Mac properly for correcting your bad behavior."

Not sure what to do she went over to him and kissed him passionately on the lips. When she finally pulled away, she was breathing heavily. "Sorry Master for not trusting you."

"All is forgiven kitten. We'll work on things as we go forward, let me just tell you up front kitten I love administering out punishment."

While she watched, her men put their shorts and t-shirts back. She noticed again no underwear. They had already said easy access. Must be why they liked going commando. She still had a whole lot to learn about the kinky lifestyle that surrounded the town of Crave. She had the rest of her life to learn, experience and enjoy. All she would do was take each day at a time. Riding out the waves, soaring in the sky above with her two men.

She couldn't wait to tell her Aunt Trudy and the rest of town about her decision to stay in Crave, to keep the diner open, and to hopefully practice law.

CHAPTER 14

Excitement peaked her insides, once the three of them arrived at the fairgrounds. She had forgotten how big the picnic really was.

Everything was looking so festive. A large white circus tent had been set up a few days ago. Red, white, and blue table clothes lined a dozen or so picnic table under the tent. Mac took her left hand, while Dillon took her right, they spotted the large banner that read "Maxwell's Diner."

As they walked towards the banner, she started to shake a little. Her nerves were rearing to go, but as soon as they reached the roped off area and saw how everything had been neatly arranged, her nerves settled instantly. Everything was in tiptop order. The silverware bins were filled, the paper plates were neatly stacked, and a large rotisserie grill had several chickens spinning around. A large fire pit, with a pig roasting was filling the area with a succulent smell.

ABIGAIL LEE JUSTICE

Everyone had pulled together to make her parents memory long lasting. After her parents died, the townspeople had come to Charlie and asked if she would still be doing the Fourth of July picnic. At first, she was reluctant, but now seeing how the town had banned together, she had nothing but love for everyone that she has so desperately pushed away. She would make sure that this picnic would go on for a long as she still had a living breath in her lungs.

Her two guys told her that they were going to help their parents bring thing from their cars. Just when she was about to cry, her aunt came up from behind her with a basket full of flowers. As always, her aunt had an eye for decorations. She loved to use everything natural when making centerpieces for the table.

"I see you're looking much better today sweetheart, A little rest did you well."

"I'm feeling so rejuvenated. What can I do to help?'

"Let's see, why don't you go say hi to Judge Johnson, he's over talking to Bryce Felts and Lexi Blackston. You remember them don't you?"

"Oh my God. I haven't seen those two for years."

"Their doing a demo tonight at The FARM."

"Really."

"Yep they drove down form Baltimore this morning and are planning on spending the night."

A crazy notion crossed Charlie's mind was Mac and Dillon planning on going to The FARM tonight and if so would they be taking her. After talking about the lifestyle for the past twenty-four hours, she sort of regretted that she still had so much to learn. She remembered that Dillon had said to her earlier "We're going to take one day at a time."

Her aunt pushed her over to where her friends were talking with the judge. As soon as Lexi spotted her she took off running for her friend, both girls embraced each other. It had been six years since she last seen then face to face. So much had changed since then, even though she kept up with Lexi on social media, she hadn't physically seen her in years.

This was another chance for Charlie to heal form the inside by re-establishing a friendship with Lexi. Lisa Phillips, Charlie's therapist had told her yesterday to reach out to people you once loved and trusted. And Lexi was one of those people.

Surprised to see how happy Lexi looked with Bryce, this was how she hoped she could be with Mac and Dillon. After talking for a few minutes with the judge, Bryce and Lexi, Charlie knew that she needed to get Lexi away from the guys for just a few minutes so that she could pepper her with questions about the lifestyle, lucky for Charlie she heard in the distance Justine calling both of their names.

"Hey, bitches! Starting the party without me?" Justine shouted.

"Damn woman you get more beautiful every day now that you're pregnant."

"Shut your trap, bitch, eight more weeks and the gremlins taking up residency in my womb will show their bright faces."

Justine was seven months pregnant with triplets; she had been a lucky girl to tie down the Murphy brothers a year ago. Now look at her she was about to start her own happy family.

"Hey don't talk about my godchildren like that; you know they can hear you right."

"Did you just call them your godchildren, woman?"

Charlie had tears in her eyes when she shook her head yes. "I can't think of a better day than to tell you that I'm staying in Crave and yes I can't wait to be your babies' godmother, if you'll still have me."

"Still have you, we never got rid of you. I knew you'd come around one day." Justine took Charlie in her arms and gave her the biggest bear hung a pregnant woman could give. It had been forever since she could talk freely and openly with just the girls. She needed to get her question out before her guys made their way back over to her. It was almost a little embarrassing to start the conversation but it was now or never.

After opening up her heart and soul to both girls about things that she needed to learn or do, all three girls were giggling and having a grand old time. Like in the past girls loved to talk about boyfriends, husbands, and sex.

Going over things about The FARM, Lexi said she would have Bryce talk to Mac and Dillon during the picnic about bringing her to the demo tonight. Justine told her not to worry about clothes that she had a closet full that she hadn't put on since her pregnancy.

Before leaving for the picnic this morning both guys did tell her that they had a surprise for her this evening. She thought maybe they were planning to bring her to The FARM all along.

Gossiping for more than an hour, Charlie had one more thing that was weight her chest down, she walked over to Judge Johnson and asked if she could set up an appointment to talk about setting up a law practice in Crave County. She was shocked when he told her that he had been waiting for her to take the plunge and that all she had to do was call and talk to Madge his secretary.

With a bit of pep in her step, everyone made their way back over under the large tent. Looking around she searched for the two guys that had her feeling alive, when she spotted them she ran to their sides. Both guys took her in their arms. She looked into their eyes and the look they had made her heart pitter patter in her chest. She loved the feeling when they were together. Funny how before she loved being separated from life, now she could get enough of human contact.

"I missed both of you."

"You did baby."

"I did. Did you find your parents?"

"We did. They'll be over in just a few moments. My mom said she's excited to see you."

"Me too." Her eyes must have shown them how excited she was when they each squeezed her tighter in their grips.

"Did you tell your parents about me?"

"Well let's just say we told them we have the best keep secret in all of Crave."

"You told them what?" She shook her head with a slight little grim on her face. She was their best keep secret and that excited her. Before she got a chance to say anything else she heard Doc ask for everyone's attention. The crowd under the tent was filled with family, and friends. Knowing what the doc was about to do, tears welled in her eyes, not out of sadness but out of happiness that her aunt would finally be surrounded by love form her new family.

Once the crowd heard the proposal, shouts of joy were heard under the tent. She ran to her aunt's side and hugged her with every ounce of happiness that she had within her soul.

Feeling her guys on hands on her back, each one tapped her shoulder making her turn around. At the same time, both guys dropped to their knees. Reaching for her hands Mac took her right and Dillon took her left, each guys held up a small jewelry box.

"Charlotte Maxwell, I fell in love with you back in high school but being the cool guy, I let you slip through my fingers and didn't see you for who you were. I saw you as unapproachable. When you left for college I knew that you would be back someday, I just didn't know when. When I saw you for the first time yesterday I knew you were mine. Will you marry me and make me the happiest man in the whole wide world. I told you my heart belongs to you."

Before she could answer his question, she heard Dillon words. "Charlotte Maxwell, I fell in love with you at Jackson Hole years ago, I let my pride work its way in between us, I knew that someday our paths would meet again and they did yesterday. My heart only belongs to you. Will you marry me and make me the happiest man in the whole wide world except for Mac? We want nothing more to make you ours forever."

Tears of joy ran down her face as both guys waited at her feet. The entire time she stood in front of her family and friends she kept looking for the sign from above that her parents would have wanted this for her. She remembered the picture above her parents' bed and the same one above the Master bedroom in Mac and Dillon's house. This had been her sign from her mother; she bet every family had the same sign above their beds.

"Happiness isn't about getting what you want all the time. It's about loving what you have and being grateful for it." At that moment she knew, her happiness was

staring up at her, her two men were on their knees asking her to trust them. It was now or never.

"Yes, I will marry you, Mackenzie Ryder, and I will marry you too, Dillon Ryder."

Shouts of happiness were heard as loud as the church bells rang on a Sunday morning service. She felt them slip a ring on her left index finger. She looked down and saw the ring that her mother had worn. Her father's gave it to her mother when they proposed so many years ago.

"How did you get my mother's ring?"

"Your aunt had it for safe keeping. When I talked to your aunt this morning and asked her for your hand in marriage, she said she had something that was left for you when it came time for you to get married. Your aunt had it locked up for safekeeping; I had her bring it with her. She was pretty sure that you would want it."

"We have something else for you baby." It was a second ring that Dillon placed on the same finger "This was our grandmother's ring. It was passed down to us, to give to the wife that we shared. And only with the wife we shared."

Both guys got up off their knees, they took turns kissing and twirling their girl around. She couldn't believe how yesterday she had nothing and today she was the happiest girl in Crave County. Life has its ups and down and no matter how you look at life sometimes it's better to face things with more than one lonely heart, and in this case, she was facing life with three bonded hearts.

EPILOGUE
TWO MONTHS LATER

The sun was shining, the birds were chirping, a large tent had been erected in the same spot as the Fourth of July picnic. Today was no picnic, instead elegant crisp white table cloths covered round tables, topped with fresh bouquets of flowers, sparkling white and silver plates sat at every place setting. Red and black foiled heart shaped chocolates were scattered around the tables. Strands of wedding bell lights had been twisted around the beams holding up the large tent. Bright Mylar balloons were scattered throughout the area with saying of congratulations, just married, love, and happiness.

When the Ryder twins proposed to Charlie on July 4th, they originally wanted to get married the following week, but Charlie put her foot down and said if she was going to get married to both of them she wanted to wait until after Justine delivered her babies. Most likely it was

Justine who said that she wasn't standing at Charlie's side like a big swollen balloon.

And seeing how Charlie had both of her men twisted around her little finger, what she said always worked in her favor. She still got punished for having a pouty, mouthy, bratty side, which had come out in the past few weeks. She was showing her true submissive sides.

Standing at the entrance to the tent in her floor length pearl white, empire waist wedding gown, holding a bouquet of fresh wildflowers, tied with a steel grey ribbon, Charlie scanned the entire room taking in the ambiance.

Her eyes spotted her two men standing in their grey pinned stripe tuxedos. Judge Johnson stood in the center of the room in his black robe, Doc Johnson who would soon be her uncle in a few months, stood to the right of her grooms.

On the bride's side, Justine blushed as she blew kisses to her three Neanderthal looking men, each holding a baby carrier. Justine's majestic long tapered silver gown showed off her beautiful figure. She looked absolutely radiant after giving birth to two boys and a little girl two weeks before.

Next to Justine stood a glowing Gloria in a strapless silver chiffon dress who couldn't keep her eyes off Greg and his cousin Curtis who were sitting in the second row on the bride's side. Curtis had moved to Crave a few months back and was now managing Maxwell's Diner soon to be Maxwell-Ryder Diner once they said their I dos.

Sitting in the first row on the bride's side was a tearful set of aunts who hadn't stopped crying since all of the wedding festivities started a week ago. Next to them were three empty chairs with three single red roses wrapped with a silver bow where her parent would have sat. On the groom's side was Gloria her new mother in law with the biggest smile on her face.

Scanning the rest of the tent, she saw her friend Kyle Zellar and his new fiancée Sophie, from Baltimore. Next to them, she saw Lexi holding hands with her boyfriend Blake. Everyone had pitched together making her special day a joyous one.

Taking one final look around the tent, seeing the happiness in everyone's faces, had tears streaming down her cheeks.

Before the wedding march started, her two new fathers-in-law to be, walked up to her one on each side, each one whispered something in her ear making her giggle.

Hearing the traditional wedding march play brought a tear to her eyes. The moment had finally come where she no longer felt like damaged goods; instead, she felt like the princess her men saw in her.

Walking down the aisle with her two fathers-in-law she finally reached her two waiting grooms. Colton lifted her veil and kissed her on her right cheek, while Dustin did the same thing on her left cheek. Each father took her hands and joined them with their sons.

She gracefully accepted the hands of her men, and stood before God, friends and family members as they committed themselves to one another.

When it came time for them to say the "I dos" there wasn't a dry eye under the entire tent. Once Judge Johnson finally announced them as Mr. Mackenzie Ryder and Mr. Dillon Ryder and Mrs. Charlotte Maxwell-Ryder each of the grooms took their turn at kissing their bride. Everyone shouted cheers of joy as bells rang. Butterflies and doves were released to signify the happy joining of three more deserving people.

Life for Charlie had drastically changed in the past few months. She no longer viewed herself as the curvy, redheaded girl who had no purpose in life, instead she saw herself as a courageous survivor with the sole purpose to live in the moment and be as happiest as she could be.

The End.

AUTHOR'S NOTE

I hope I have wet your appetite and stirred your imagination with Lucky 13. Coming in February 2017, Volume 2 of Lucky 13 will take you on another journey with a brand new set of Doms, and more fantasies that will arouse your desires.

Don't forget, if you want to be a part of my street team Abigail's Angels on Facebook all you need to do is send me a message to that account.

Happy Reading

XOXO

Abigail

OTHER BOOKS BY ABIGAIL

Bound by her Master: Book 1 in The Heart Series.

Sophie Spencer is a happily married, twenty-nine year old cardiologist. Suddenly her world is shattered to pieces. The love of her life, her only love, is taken from her in a devastating car accident. Stricken with grief, depression, and loneliness for the past two years, Sophie takes the advice of a close friend to venture down a new path – exploring the inner sides of submission. Not knowing what it truly means to submit, Sophie indulges her desires by visiting a prominent BDSM club on her own. Could she fully submit to another man's will, or was the bond that she shared with her husband unbreakable? That's the question Sophie must come to terms with.

Kyle Zeller is one hundred percent Alpha male. He owns a high end BDSM club, but has not been in a serious relationship for over a year. Serious skeletons that are buried deep in the back of Kyle's mind keeps holding him back from making a true commitment, which is until Sophie Spencer walks into the Cellar. Kyle see's for the first time in his life the person he's been looking for, she standing in front of him. He already knows everything about Sophie's past, including her desires to submit. Will Kyle's past resurface and shatter this potential relationship too?

Second Chances: Book 2 in the Heart Series

Knowing that happily-ever-afters only happen in fairy tales, Sophie Spencer spends an amazing night with her Prince Charming. Being new to the lifestyle, she allows her hidden fears to take over and does the unthinkable. She screams her safe-word...and runs directly into danger. Will her moment of weakness cause her world to be torn apart again? Or will she overcome her trust issues and fully surrender to her Prince.

Falling in love had been the furthest thing from Kyle Zellar's mind, but when Sophie Spencer fully submits to his dominant demands, his only recourse is to claim her as his. Before he can claim her, he is forced to let her go.

Fighting his inner demons and past issues of childhood abandonment, he knows he must sort out his own life before he can move on with his future.

But will it be too little too late?

Author's note: This is the second book in The Heart Series, and NOT a standalone. You, of course, can read them in any order you like, but I would recommend you read Bound By Her Master first.

Theirs To Love: Book 1 Doms of Crave County

One curvy, redheaded attorney; two sexy twins. Sometimes you must face your demons head on... Determined to forget a dark secret in her past, Charlotte Maxwell left home when she turned eighteen, immersed herself in textbooks, and eventually launched a successful career as a prominent New York attorney. Isolating herself from family, friends and co-workers, she allows depression, fear, and most of all sexual tension to build up inside her, mind, body, and soul.

Eight years later, she's forced to return to her hometown of Crave County, where everyone lives some sort of kinky lifestyle, her parents being amongst the many. Tasked with adjudicating her parents' estate after their unfortunate deaths, Charlotte's hidden demons begin to resurface and along with her attraction for two of the hottest businessmen ever to steam up a room.

Mackenzie and Dillon Ryder were born and raised in Crave County. Practicing what the town preaches has always been a part of who they are. Despite their mutual cravings for the feisty redhead, they have always considered Charlotte Maxwell off limits. These two sexual dominates have been searching for their missing puzzle piece since high school. No submissive has come close to completing their circle, not until Charlotte needs them to rescue her. Not only is she the answer they've been looking for, but she too has been secretly pining for them. Will fate bring these three together, or will their insecurities separate them for good?

Ours To Love: Book 2 Doms of Crave County

One curvy, blonde waitress; One sexy chef; One hot restaurant manager. Together they make a recipe for love!

Gloria Jean Fitzpatrick carries a dark horse not only etched within her mind, but branded on her skin as a permanent reminder of the abuse she has suffered. After ending a three year long abusive D/s relationship, she believes her days of submission are over.

Heart broken, wounded, and alone, she devotes her waking hours to taking care of her disabled brother, working crazy shifts at the local diner, and over indulging in life's finest pleasures, sweets.

Carefully guarding her heart, Gloria watches as her two closest male friends continue to dominate other submissives. Dreaming of much more than friendship, she makes the hardest decision of her life, but will her hidden demons hold her back?

Greg and Curtis O'Malley are no strangers to the art of domination and have been dominating willing submissives together for years. Life for these two sexy cousins has surely had its ups and downs. Dishing up savory meals at Maxwell Diner is only one of Greg O'Malley special gifts, his other... dominating a willing submissive.

Escaping the big city to manage Maxwell Diner was a life changing move for Curtis O'Malley. Now his quest to find the perfect submissive to complete his and George's nexus may finally be over, but will Gloria's past come back to haunt their happiness?

The Doms of Crave County series contains mature themes including heart pounding action, suspense, graphic violence, and a lot of steamy hot sex with multiple partners.

ABOUT THE AUTHOR

Abigail Lee Justice writes emotional, erotic, romantic suspense that includes a BDSM theme. She creates strong characters who seem real but are flawed in some ways; some couples Happily Ever After will be a work in process. Some characters' problems are just too steamy to fix in one book.

Born and raised in Baltimore City by two wonderful, supportive, loving parents, as a child Abigail made up vivid tales in her head. Until one day, a friend told her instead of keeping her stories locked her head she needed to put them on paper and that's exactly what she did.

Abigail met her husband thirty years ago on a blind date (thanks Dan C.) while working a part time job to put herself through college. She fell madly in love with her Prince Charming and has been since the first day they met.

By day, Abigail practices medicine in a busy Cardiologist practice. By evening, she switches her white coat for more relaxed comfortable clothing. She has two wonderful adult sons and a very spoiled chocolate lab. In the wee hours of the night, she writes BDSM romances. In her spare time when not working or writing, Abigail enjoys reading, concocting vegetarian dishes, scuba diving, high adventure activities, living in the lifestyles she writes about, and doing lots and lots of research making sure her characters get it just right. If you'd like to become part of Abigail's street team or become a beta reader for future books, drop her a message on FB@abigailleejustice or visit her website @ www.abigailleejustice.com

Made in the USA
Middletown, DE
11 September 2019